DEFINITELY DAISY

Watch Out, Daisy

Jenny Oldfield

Three exciting Definitely Daisy stories:

You're a Disgrace, Daisy!

Just You Wait, Winona!

You Must be Joking, Jimmy!

Hodder Children's Books

A division of Hodder Headline Limited

'A big thanks to the hundreds of
kids in dozens of schools who helped me bring Daisy to life.'

First published in Great Britain as 3 separate books in 2001
by Hodder Children's Books

This edition published in 2005

2 4 6 8 10 9 7 5 3 1

A Catalogue record for this book is available from
the British Library

ISBN 0 340 89323 0

Typeset by Ana Molina

Printed and bound in Great Britain by
Bookmarque Ltd, Croydon, Surrey

The paper and board used in this paperback by Hodder Children's Books are
natural recyclable products made from wood grown in sustainable forests.
The manufacturing processes conform to the environmental regulations
of the country of origin.

Hodder Children's Books
a division of Hodder Headline Ltd
338 Euston Road
London NW1 3BH

You're a disgrace, Daisy!

Jenny Oldfield

Illustrated by
Lauren Child

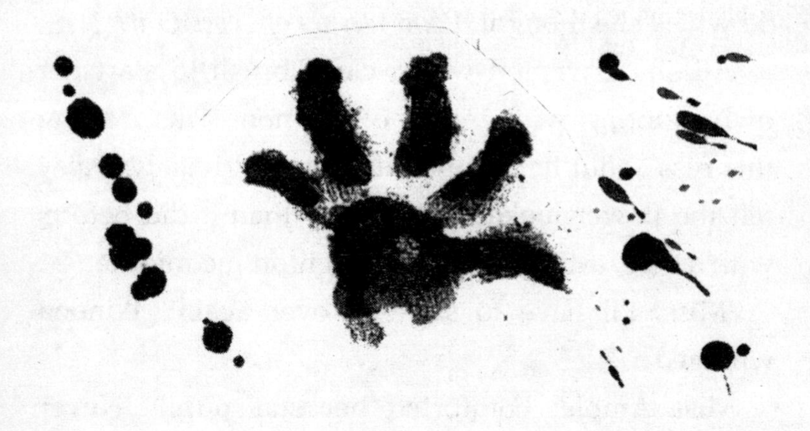

One

'Daisy Morelli, watch out for the wet . . . paint! Oh dear!'

Miss Ambler's warning came too late. Daisy had reached over the art table for a clean brush and smudged Winona's beautiful picture.

'Please, Miss, Daisy spoiled my sunflower!' Winona wailed.

The teacher came across the classroom to inspect the damage.

'I know she did, dear. And she ruined her nice clean school shirt as well.'

Daisy stared down at the yellow paint on her chest.

Then she wiped her sticky hand on her dark grey skirt.

'Don't do that, Daisy!' Miss Ambler shrieked.

Too late again. Daisy's skirt now matched her shirt. So what? she thought. *Paint washes off, doesn't it?*

All she'd wanted was a clean brush to start her own painting with. And now Winona was making this fuss about her stupid sunflower. Privately, Daisy felt the flower looked better now than it did before, with a nice, artistic handprint right in the middle.

'Miss, I'll have to start all over again!' Winona whinged.

Miss Ambler comforted her star pupil. 'Never mind, dear. Why don't you tidy up and then help me take down the old pictures from the wall? Daisy

Morelli, you can stay in during playtime and scrub the art table for being so careless.'

Winona's whinge changed to a smug smile. She tossed her long, fair curls at a scowling Daisy. 'Serves you right!' she whispered.

'What did I do?' Daisy asked, turning to her best friend, Jimmy Black.

Jimmy carried on sploshing yellow paint across his paper. *Sploosh – sploosh – dabble – dabble – splosh!*

Daisy forgot her troubles with smarmy Winona. 'Hey, that doesn't look anything *like* what it's supposed to look like!'

Splosh – sploosh – squiggle – stab! Jimmy painted on.

'It's more like a custard pie than a sunflower!'

Squiggle – squiggle. 'Don't care!' Jimmy replied.

Miss Ambler came by with a small metal stepladder, closely followed by Winona. 'Very nice, Jimmy dear,' she murmured. Then the teacher frowned hard and told Daisy off again. 'Come away from Jimmy's table, Daisy Morelli. If I've told you once, I've told you a thousand times; don't interfere with other people's work!'

'Daisy, leave Nathan's spider jar alone!'

Playtime had come and gone. Scrubbing the art table had added red, blue and green splodges to the yellow stains on Daisy's shirt and skirt. And missing the playtime soccer challenge had put her in a really bad mood.

'We won, four-nil!' Jimmy had whispered, as he slid into the seat next to Daisy's. His face was red and sweaty, his football shirt ripped at the shoulder. But he was happy.

'Don't tell me, I don't want to know!' Daisy had moaned, giving Winona the dead eye.

And now it was Science, and she was in trouble with Miss Ambler again.

All she'd done was take a pencil and get ready to poke Legs, the fat black spider Nathan Moss kept as a pet. Winona Smarmy Jones had watched her do it, then run off to report her to the teacher.

'I'm not even touching him!' Daisy pleaded her innocence and hid the pencil behind her back.

'Miss, she nearly did!' Winona claimed. 'I saw Legs trying to run away and hide!'

How could a spider hide in an empty jam-jar? Daisy scowled at Winona, the teacher's pet. Mizz Neat-and-Petite, with her golden curls and ironed shirts.

And now Nathan came and whisked his precious spider to safety. 'I hope he escapes from his jar and gives you a poison-bite!' he hissed.

Weird Nathan who never bothered to tie his shoe laces. Nathan who knew everything about spiders and nothing about football. Like, seriously weird!

Daisy refused to be scared. 'Legs doesn't bite. He's cute.'

'Yuck!' Winona whispered to her curly-haired neighbour, Leonie Flowers. 'Daisy thinks creepy Legs is cute!'

Leonie carried on with her amazing drawing of a spider's web. The thin black lines formed a neat network on the white page. 'Me too,' she murmured. 'He's all soft and furry . . .'

So Winona flounced off to join Nathan. And Daisy stayed in Miss Ambler's bad books.

One hour later, Daisy was out of the classroom on a mission.

'Come away from that pond!' A loud voice made her jump. She staggered, tottered, then stepped into the shallow water.

Mr King, the school caretaker, came rushing up. His pet bulldog, Fat Lennox, panted along behind him. 'I said, mind you don't fall in!' he cried. Too late again.

'Miss Ambler sent me to collect pond-weed for our Science lesson,' she explained. The teacher's idea had been to give Daisy a job to do to keep her out of trouble. Only, here she was, getting told off again.

Squelch! When she lifted her foot out of the pond and put it down on the grass, her trainer oozed muddy water.

Bernie King took no notice of Daisy's lame excuse. 'A likely story!' he fumed, looming large, keys to every door in the school hanging in a bunch from his belt. 'No teacher with a grain of sense would send you on a tricky errand like that!' The caretaker didn't like Daisy. Or Jimmy, or Leonie – in fact, he was probably in the wrong job, since he frankly didn't like kids, full-stop.

Daisy backed away. She forgot that the pond was behind her. Only when she stumbled into the weeds and mud again, then sat down in the cold water with a bump, did she remember where she was.

'Didn't I try to warn you?' King grunted. 'I said, stay away from that pond!'

Daisy stared down at her own sorry figure. She was

wet. Her shoes were muddy. Her clothes were covered in paint. This had *not* been a good day.

'Daisy, don't you dare go near the baby looking like that!'

Angie Morelli waited at the school gates for her daughter. She gasped in horror as Daisy ran to paw her chubby little sister with muddy, paint-smeared hands.

'Aah, goo-goo-goo! Chobble-chobble, wibble-wobble!' Winona Jones was there first, poking her nose in and cooing over Mia's push-chair. She picked up a pink stuffed rabbit from the pavement and handed it back, goo-gooing and choo-chooing all over again.

'Goo-goo-goo!' Mia chortled back.

Meanwhile, Jimmy and Leonie sped by.

'Race you to the bus-stop!' Leonie challenged.

Jimmy nodded, took the corner with a screech of pretend-brakes, then legged it down the street. Daisy bet herself five pounds that Jimmy, who could run like a whippet, would win the race.

'Daisy, you're a disgrace,' Angie grumbled wearily. 'What did I do to deserve a daughter like you?'

'"Daisy, you're a disgrace!"' Daisy mimicked behind her mum's back, while Angie sighed, then turned to talk to another mother.

Winona stepped in smartly. 'I *saw* that!' she hissed.

'So?' Daisy was fed-up. She'd had enough. More

than enough. Too much, in fact. So she jutted out her chin and faced up to Win-oh-stupid-nah. 'What you gonna do about it?'

'Daisy, don't argue!' Angie Morelli said sharply, glancing over her shoulder.

'Daisy – Daisy – Daisy – don't – don't – don't!' First from Miss Rambler-Ambler and Bernie King. Now from her mum. 'Don't do that, Daisy. Daisy, you're a disgrace!' She was sick of it.

So sick that she would . . . she would . . . well, she might even explode. Right here, right now, on this pavement. She fizzed and sparked inside, fidgeting and feeling the pressure build up.

'Daisy, what's wrong? Why has your face gone a funny colour?' Winona asked sweetly.

Mia tossed her pink rabbit out of the push-chair again. No one told *her* off.

'It's not fair!' Daisy fumed. She watched Jimmy arrive at the bus-stop ten metres ahead of Leonie, noted that she had just won five pounds from herself; a sum of money which anyway she didn't have.

'Why is it always me?'

'Because it always is you!' Winona replied with deadly logic. 'I mean, face it, Daisy, if there's trouble around, you're going to be in the thick of it! Like, *definitely*!'

Definitely Daisy pulled a sour face and stuck out her tongue.

'Daisy, that's not nice!' (Her mum had eyes in the back of her head, of course.)

'It's true!' Winona insisted. Then she wormed her way into Mrs Morelli's conversation and invited herself to the Morellis' house for tea.

No, not that! Anything but that! Daisy pleaded silently for her mum to say no.

'Of course. Daisy would love to have you, wouldn't you, Daisy?' Angie said, a steely eye fixed on her squirming daughter.

Oh no! Get me out of here! Daisy gave Winona a furious look as the small group set off down the street. *Aliens, please land in your spaceship and kidnap me! Beam me off into another dimension, take me to a distant universe. Only, please, please, don't leave me here on Woodbridge Road and make me have tea with girly, curly, pearly Winona (Call-Me-Mizz-Perfect) Jones!*

Two

'Hello, my *bambina!*' Gianni Morelli lifted Mia out of her push-chair and held her high in the air. The baby giggled and gurgled. She wiggled her fat arms and legs like a frog.

'Bambina Mia. Mia bambina!' The proud dad laughed and tossed the baby. Then he took her off into the kitchen, where he was busy cooking pizzas.

Daisy and Mia's dad ran an Italian restaurant on Duke Street called the Pizza Palazzo. He was always laughing, always tossing the baby into the air.

These days he seemed not to notice Daisy.

'Put your school bag away in your room,' her mum

told her, once Winona had gobbled up a whole pizza margarita, drunk three large Cokes and waddled off home. 'Your dad will be cross if you leave it lying around in the restaurant.'

Daisy frowned. She knew for a fact that her smiley-faced dad had never been cross in his life. He just laughed his way through the days, pounding pizza-dough, chopping onions and dreaming of Italy.

'And put your school uniform in the washing-machine.' Angie Morelli continued to nag Daisy. 'How come you got into such a state at school today? Honestly, Daisy, why can't you be neat and tidy like Winona?'

Daisy waited until her mum had left the room, then stuck two fingers down her throat and made a puking sound.

'You feeling OK?' Just at that moment, Jimmy popped his head around the door. His dark brown hair was blown about by the wind, his blue football shirt was covered in mud and he held a white plastic ball under his arm.

'No!' Daisy retorted.

'Oh.' Jimmy turned to go. 'I was gonna ask if you wanted to come and play footie with us in the park . . .'

'Wait!' Daisy's amazing recovery surprised her friend. She shot out on to Duke Street, still in her

paint-spattered uniform. 'Who's playing? Whose side am I on?'

'Goal!' The cry went up from Jimmy's team as he slammed the ball into the back of the net. 'Jim-my Black! Jim-my Black!' Jimmy did a tour of the pitch, his arms in the air, allowing his team mates to slap him on the back.

'Two-one!' Daisy cried. They were five minutes into extra time after a hard-fought one-all draw. Part of the winning team, she galloped after Jimmy and flung both arms around his neck.

'Gerroff!' he protested, ducking, then elbowing her away.

She didn't care. She was happy and hot, sweaty and chanting, 'Jim-my Black!'

Their team held on to the lead in spite of Leonie's two brave efforts to level the score.

'Oooh-aaah!' Her team mates gasped, then groaned as her second shot went wide.

Leonie collapsed on to her knees in disappointment. She held her head in her hands.

Then the final whistle blew and it was all over.

'Good match!' Jimmy trotted around the pitch, which was marked out with rolled-up jackets and spare shoes. He congratulated his team and shook hands with the gallant losers. 'Bad luck, Leonie,' he muttered.

'We'll hammer you next time!' she promised, running a hand through her short curly hair, then glancing at her watch. 'Gotta go. My mum will kill me!'

And so the players went their separate ways in the setting sun, and Jimmy and Daisy walked back home to Duke Street together.

'Have you done your Science homework for tomorrow?' Jimmy asked, stopping outside his family's flat, which was above Car World, the motor spares shop.

'Nope,' Daisy replied. Homework was boring. Homework was for wimps like weird Nathan.

'Miss Ambler will kill you.'

'Don't care.' She wandered on ten yards to the Pizza Palazzo.

'Daisy Morelli, didn't I tell you to put your uniform in the wash . . .?' her mum began as soon as she set foot through the sliding - doors.

OK, so the alien spaceship hadn't landed and come to her rescue. So she was walking to school next morning without her Science project. 'Please, Miss, the baby chewed it!' was going to be her excuse. The teacher would never believe her, but so what?

'She'll make you stay behind to do extra work,' Jimmy warned, waving his own dog-eared project in her face. Somehow, the hero of last night's soccer match had also found time to write out the life cycle of the newt.

'So?' Daisy unhitched the hem of her newly-ironed shirt from the waistband of her skirt. A headline on the billboard outside the newsagents caught her eye: LOCAL HERO TO SET UP KIDS' SOCCER ACADEMY! 'Hey, look at this!'

Jimmy saw it too, then grabbed a copy of the *Helston Herald* from the pile. 'It says here that Kevin Crowe is starting a football school for the under-twelves. If you're chosen, you get to live in and learn soccer skills from the greatest goal-scorer in the Steelers, history!'

'Wow!' To Daisy this sounded too good to be true.

'Hey, you kids, put that paper down!' the newsagent yelled from inside the shop.

'Picture it!' Jimmy sighed as they walked on to school.

'Kevin Crowe is only a living football legend, that's all!'

Daisy's head was still full of the idea of the soccer school when Miss Ambler took off her glasses and groaned at her feeble excuse for not handing in her homework.

The young teacher rubbed her eyes wearily. She got up from behind her desk, snagged a thread from her flared cotton skirt on a splinter and pulled the hem loose. 'Ttt-ttt!' Her tongue clicked against her front teeth and she frowned down at her least favourite pupil. 'Daisy Morelli, you're a complete disgrace!'

'Yes, Miss Ambler.'

'Do you really expect me to believe that poor little Mia ate your homework?'

'No, Miss Ambler.'

'I should think not. This may only be my first year in teaching, but even I can spot a fake excuse when I hear one.'

Silence this time from Daisy, as she awaited her fate.

'I'm afraid you've gone too far.' Miss Ambler trembled in front of the whole class. Her voice quivered. 'I intend to speak to the head teacher about you at playtime. Unless I'm very much mistaken, Daisy Morelli, Mrs Waymann will definitely want to have a little word.'

It was morning break. For once, Daisy didn't join in with the soccer-playing gang. Instead, she daydreamed in a corner of the yard.

'*. . . And it's Daisy Morelli surging down the middle! She's dribbled past one defender, now another . . . this girl's ball skills are truly superb!' The presenter's voice rose as Daisy headed for the goalmouth. 'Yes, she's drawn the goalkeeper out, she's flicked the ball past him and now she's* *shooting with that famous left foot . . . Slam, into the corner of the net!'*

It was the winning goal of the FA Cup final. Wembley roared. Fans spilled on to the pitch. After the match, the presenter interviewed her.

'So, Daisy, tell us, who's behind your soccer success story?'

Blushing, Daisy thanked her mother and father, her friend, Jimmy Black, and most of all, the great Kevin Crowe.

'I understand that you attended his famous Academy for the Under-Twelves?' The presenter reminded twenty million TV viewers of Daisy Morelli's footballing roots.

She beamed at the camera, then spoke. 'Yeah, thank you, Kevin. Without you, I'd be a footballing nobody . . .'

'Waymann wants a word,' Leonie dashed up to break into Daisy's dream and pass on a message. 'She says to go to her office right now.'

Daisy nodded. Hands behind her back, head down and heart thumping, she made her way into school.

Up the steps to the executioner's block. 'Do you have any final requests?' 'Yes. Tell my mum and dad I'm sorry.' Whoosh! The axe descended as Daisy knocked on Mrs Waymann's door.

'Enter!' The head teacher's voice sounded stern.

Daisy shuffled in.

Mrs Waymann looked up from writing reports, her

plump face serious. She shifted her weight, giving off a cloud of flowery perfume. 'Ah yes, Daisy Morelli. Miss Ambler would like me to have a little word . . .'

* * *

'What did she say?' Jimmy quizzed Daisy on their way home from school.

It was Friday; the end of the worst week in Daisy's life.

Pull-yourself-together. Smarten-up. Tell-the-truth. Daisy gave Jimmy the lowdown on her lousy interview with the head teacher. Oh, and, *'You simply must stop living in a fantasy world.'* Plus, *'Daisy Morelli, you're a headache.' And, 'Daisy, you attract trouble like a magnet.'*

Mrs Waymann might *look* plump and cuddly sitting in her cloud of perfume, but appearances weren't always what they seemed.

'Daisy-Disaster-Morelli' was what she'd called her, before finally deciding that there was no way around it; she, Mrs Waymann, would be obliged to write to Daisy's parents about their daughter's poor behaviour in school.

'Phew, bad news!' Jimmy whistled. 'What you gonna do?'

'Run away from home,' Daisy told him, matter of factly. She'd already got it all planned out in her head.

'Are you serious?' Jimmy's jaw nearly hit the pavement.

'Where are you gonna run to?'

'It's a secret.'

'Yeah, but you can tell me. I'm Jimmy, remember; your best mate!'

Daisy relented. 'OK, I'm planning to pack my bag in the middle of the night tonight. I'm gonna write Mum and Dad a note, saying not to worry, I'm safe and all that. Then tomorrow, before breakfast, I'm gonna creep out of the house without anyone seeing.' As she described her secret plan, her dark eyes sparkled. This was going to be one BIG adventure.

'Yeah, but where to?' Jimmy insisted. They had

reached Duke Street and his mum was standing, arms folded, at the door of Car World, looking out for him.

'That's the really good bit,' Daisy whispered. 'The plan is, I sneak off from here and get in touch with Kevin Crowe.'

The famous name stopped Jimmy dead in his tracks. '*The* Kevin Crowe?' he stammered.

She nodded.

'What on earth for?' said a flabbergasted Jimmy.

'I want to join his Academy.' To Daisy it all made perfect sense. 'I'll learn to be a soccer superstar, and then, when I'm scoring the winning goal in the World Cup Final, everyone who ever nagged me or told me off will have to be sorry!'

'Yeah!' Jimmy's glance was admiring at first. Then he hit a serious snag, which he felt he had to point out. 'But you're a girl!'

'Yeah. So?'

'Girls don't play in the World Cup. They don't even play in the League.'

A deep frown creased Daisy's forehead. 'They soon will!' she promised. She would prove herself so gifted at heading the ball that Kevin Crowe would go along to the FA and get them to change the rules.

Jimmy took this on board. For a while he rolled his eyes thoughtfully. 'The Kevin Crowe Academy for Under-Twelves,' he muttered. Then he chucked in a casual suggestion. 'How about I run away too? I could come with you to the Academy.'

Daisy looked him in the eye. 'Seriously?'

'Jimmy, come in for your tea!' his mum called from the doorstep. 'It's bangers, chips and beans!'

Jimmy ignored her, his eyes alive with excitement. 'Truth!' he swore.

'OK!' Daisy said, swiftly making up her mind. 'Meet me tomorrow morning at the park gates, eight o'clock sharp!'

Three

No more school.

No more Miss Ambler shrieking, 'Daisy, you're a disgrace!' No more miserable Bernie King jangling his keys, shaking his head and saying, 'Sorry, no can do!'

Curled up in bed that night, Daisy thought of all the things she wouldn't miss.

No more homework – cool. And none of that naggy stuff from the dinner ladies about washing your hands before you ate your dinner.

Hey, and no more tidying her classroom drawer!

Uh-oh! Suddenly Daisy gasped, then sat bolt upright in bed. She'd just remembered Herbie.

Herbie was her squidgy, furry golden hamster and she'd left him behind in her drawer. Not just for the weekend, as it happened, but forever.

'What's the matter, love? Why aren't you asleep?' Daisy's mum poked her head around the bedroom door.

'I forgot Herbie!' she wailed. He would be lonely and scared in that dark drawer, amongst her broken crayons and crumpled worksheets.

Angie Morelli smiled. 'Is that all? I thought it was something serious.'

'It is! I never leave Herbie behind. He doesn't like being by himself.'

'Hmm.' Daisy's mum came to sit on the edge of the bed. 'You don't think you're making a bit too much of this? Herbie isn't a real hamster, remember. He's only a soft toy.'

'Only!' Daisy squeaked. 'I've had him since I was little!'

OK, so he was half-bald and squidgy from going through the washing-machine too many times. And maybe he did only have one eye and these days his colour wasn't exactly golden. But, uncool as it sounded, Herbie was still her special hamster. And the closest Daisy had ever come to a real live pet.

'Do you know where you left him?' Angie asked kindly.

'In my drawer.'

'That's OK, then. He'll still be there on Monday.'

But I won't! Daisy frowned, then slid back down under her duvet to hide her face. She mustn't let her mum suspect what she and Jimmy were planning.

'Better now?'

'Mm.' (Close eyes, pretend to be sleepy.)

'Good. Sleep well.' Angie stood up and tiptoed out. 'Good night, Daisy!'

No reply from the hump in the bed. Daisy produced a couple of loud snores for effect. She heard the light switch on the landing flick off and her mum's footsteps go quietly downstairs.

'Listen, Jimmy, we have to go to school!'

Daisy's announcement at eight o'clock next morning came as a shock. 'B-b-but!' he stammered. 'It's Saturday. Anyway, I thought we were running away!'

'We are. It's just I need to fetch Herbie.'

'Fetch Herbie?' Jimmy echoed. He shifted his half-empty rucksack from one shoulder to the other. The bag contained only a spare football kit, a toothbrush and a signed photo of Robbie Exley, the Steelers' ace goal scorer. 'Do we have to?'

Daisy nodded. 'Think of the one thing you would never leave behind . . .' She waited for him to suggest something.

'My Robbie Exley pic.' There was no doubt in Jimmy's mind. He'd rather die than be separated from Super-Rob.

'Right. So you'd go back to school to collect him if you'd left him behind, wouldn't you?' she asked with a piercing look.

'OK.' He gave in and agreed to head for Woodbridge Road, still coming up with reasons not to as they drew near. 'It's not a week day. What if school's locked?'

'It won't be. There's a netball match. They have to open the building so kids can use the changing-rooms.' Daisy had thought all this through during the night. And poor Herbie had been at the front of her mind all the time she was secretly packing and saying goodbye to sleeping baby Mia.

Goodbye, Mi-mi! Goodbye, bedroom! Goodbye, Mum and Dad (who had been busy stacking shelves in the restaurant store-room.) Then finally, *Goodbye, Pizza Palazzo*!

That had been the tough bit; knowing that you would never see your home and family again. Or at least, not until you became a sporting hero and returned in triumph on the open topped, Cup-winners double-decker bus.

Daisy had slid out of the door on to the street, her

bag on her back, her heart heavy. She'd even shed a tear over Mia and slipped a passport-sized photograph of herself under the baby's pillow so that Mia wouldn't forget her older sister. Then she'd propped the farewell note to her parents against the microwave and beaten a hasty retreat.

Maybe Jimmy won't show up, she thought, as she nipped around the side of Car World and headed for their meeting place at the park gates. In which case, I could change my mind about running away to Kevin Crowe's Football Academy after all.

But Jimmy was already there in his newest bright blue football strip which was a little bit too big.

So she had to go through with the plan. But, before they set off to look for Kevin Crowe's place, she had to rescue Herbie.

'We'll have to sneak in without being seen,' Jimmy whispered as the school gates came into view.

'Yoo-hoo, Jimmy! Yoo-hoo, Daisy!' Winona Jones called from across the street.

She was taking her fancy pet poodle, Lulu, for a walk. The curly-haired white dog trotted along beside her neat owner, ears pricked, pom-pom tail poked straight up in the air.

'Ohhh . . . no!' Daisy and Jimmy groaned.

Winona and Lulu crossed the street to join them. 'I didn't know you played netball, Jimmy!' she joked.

'Ha-ha,' he said crossly.

'Very funny,' Daisy chipped in.

'So what are you two doing here?' Winona eyed their rucksacks suspiciously.

Quick-thinking Daisy gave the reply. 'We came to watch Leonie.'

'You're loads too early.' Glancing at her watch, Winona made it clear that she thought they were up to something.

'Yeah, we're here to help make the orange juice and

biscuits for half-time,' Jimmy lied, his freckled face burning bright red.

'Hey, me too!' Winona sounded pleased that she wasn't the only helper.

Trust Mizz Perfect, Mizz Teacher's Pet to offer to help Miss Ambler on a non-school day. Daisy cringed.

Winona was positively bubbling with excitement. 'Wait here for me while I take Lulu home, OK? I'll only be five minutes. Then we can all go into school together.'

So Jimmy and Daisy stood by helplessly while Winona scooted off down the road. But as soon as she

turned the corner, they zoomed across the empty playground towards the main door.

'See, it's locked!' Jimmy sighed after he'd rattled and turned the handle in vain.

'Sshh, here comes Bernie!' Daisy spotted the stout figure of the caretaker crossing the yard from his house. His keys jangled as usual, and he was armed with a metal bucket full of steaming water plus a long-handled mop. Fat Lennox followed close behind Daisy and Jimmy ducked down behind two giant flower tubs until Bernie and his bulldog had passed by.

'I dunno, kids these days!' he grumbled to

himself. 'They don't know they're born. They have it too easy; someone to drive them to school, someone to drive them home again. In my day you had to walk, come rain, come shine . . .' He muttered on as he put down his mop and bucket by the entrance. Then he gave a loud sigh as he unhooked his keys to open the door.

From behind her flower tub, Daisy gave Jimmy a thumbs-up signal. In a few seconds, after they'd given the caretaker time to stomp off down the corridor, she and Jimmy would be able to sneak in after him.

'In my day, you did a paper-round before breakfast, then you walked into school,' Bernie reminded himself. 'Kids today are too soft by half . . .'

Jimmy and Daisy watched him pick up his clanking bucket and go on his way. Then they darted into the school, past the Welcome board outside the secretary's office, and down the corridor into their own classroom.

Once inside, Daisy dived straight for her drawer. She pulled it out and rummaged amongst the rubbish, spilling felt-tips down the back and throwing her history project on castles on to the floor. At last she found what she was looking for.

'Herbie!' she cried, pulling out a squished, dirty-brown soft toy.

The hamster's one remaining eye seemed to wink at

her as she brought him out into the light.

'C'mon, Daisy, let's get out of here!' Jimmy urged from the doorway. 'I can hear Bernie coming back!'

Clank-clank-clank went Bernie King's bucket. His keys *chink-chinked* as he walked.

So she stuffed Herbie into her bag and sprinted with Jimmy back down the corridor before the caretaker had time to reappear.

'Close!' Jimmy breathed.

'Yoo-hoo, you two!' a voice called from the gate.

'Oh no!' Daisy had forgotten about Winona. She screeched to a halt and looked for a different way out of the playground.

'I thought you said you'd wait for me,' Winona protested, making a neat run to cut off their retreat.

'That's not the way *I* remember it!' Jimmy said darkly.

(*Reasons to hate Winona Jones*; Daisy made a list.

One: *Because she's always neat and curly-girly.*

Two: *Because she's a teacher's pet.*

Three: *Because she owns Lulu, a real live pet, not just a toy.*

Four: *Because she always asks stupid questions . . .)*

'What have you got in that bag, Daisy? Why didn't you wait like you said? And Jimmy, what are you doing helping out at a netball match instead of playing footie in the park?'

Daisy was still looking for an escape. But now the

side exit was blocked by the arrival of Miss Ambler's rattling, rusting orange VW Beetle. The teacher had obviously shown up on her day off to take charge of the girls' netball match. Worse still, Winona was nipping across the playground to speak to her.

'Please, Miss, Daisy Morelli and Jimmy Black are going to help me with the refreshments!' she announced in a loud voice.

A startled Miss Ambler almost dropped the pile of netball shirts she was carrying. 'That's news to me,' she said with a quick glance at the shifty pair.

'Quick!' Daisy hissed. She'd decided that the best way out of this emergency was over the playground wall.

She and Jimmy shinned up it and were balanced on the top when Bernie King stormed out of the school.

'Hey you!' The caretaker steamrollered towards them, arms waving, voice raised to a bellow. Fat Lennox barked behind him.

'Get down off that wall before you do yourselves an injury!'

While Daisy judged the five foot drop on to the pavement below, Jimmy took off. He landed commando-style, rolling on to his side, then springing on to his feet. 'All clear!' he yelled back at Daisy, still teetering on top of the wall. So she jumped to join him.

Crouching low, bags bumping against their backs,

they skirted the playground, back towards busy Woodbridge Road.

'What now?' Jimmy hissed, pinning himself against the wall as he reached the corner.

'We catch a bus into town and start looking for the Kevin Crowe Academy.' Daisy formed her plan on the spur of the moment. After all, it couldn't be hard. Everyone would have heard about the new soccer school, so all she and Jimmy needed to do was ask at the Information Office for directions. *Easy-peasy*.

'I heard that!' Winona's voice broke in.

Swivelling round, Daisy spotted the enemy crouched on the wall directly above their heads. Winona was wearing her smug, wait-till-I-tell-Miss-Ambler expression.

'So?' Jimmy answered back. 'What's wrong with us looking for the Kevin Cro... **ouch**!'

Daisy had stamped hard on his toes and was glaring at him.

Up on the wall-top, Winona's eyes narrowed. 'You two are running away, aren't you?'

'No way!' Daisy snapped.

'Definitely not!' Jimmy held his foot and hopped about.

'You are!' Winona crowed.

Daisy reached up and caught hold of her ankle.

'Don't you dare say a word!'

Winona wobbled and squeaked. 'OK!'

Daisy tugged harder. 'Promise?'

'Promise!' Winona gasped.

Giving her one last glare, Daisy let go. Winona sank back into the playground, out of sight.

Jimmy spotted a number seven bus pulling up at the nearby stop and they sprinted to catch it. Forget Winona, Miss Ambler and Bernie King. Think about the Kevin Crowe Academy and the adventure about to begin!

Four

The trouble with running away from home was that you soon got homesick, Daisy discovered.

Not that she would admit that to Jimmy, who sat quietly beside her on the front seat of the top deck of the number seven bus.

Don't be so silly! she told herself, sounding strangely like Miss Ambler. It's only half an hour since you left the note in front of the microwave. Mum and Dad won't even have had time to miss you yet!

As the bus rumbled and lurched through the Saturday morning traffic, she remembered word for word the letter she had written.

Dear Mum and Dad,
I've had ~~enuff~~ enough. I'm always getting told off and I can't take it any more. So ~~we~~ I've decided to run away. Please let the school know that I won't be coming in any more. Mrs Waymann called me Daisy Disaster Morelli so she should be pleased. The same with miss Ambler (please tell her that I did **not** Poke Legs and I'd never do anything to hurt him. I LIKE SPIDERS!!!)
And don't try to look for ~~us~~ me. Just show Mia my picture and tell her about me when she grows up.
Your loving ~~dort~~ daughter, Daisy
PS. I'm doing this totally alone, by myself, just me. no one is coming with me!!!

'Whassamatter?' Jimmy mumbled when he heard Daisy sniffle.

'Nothing!'

'Are we on the right bus?'

'Yep.' *Sniff-sniff-swallow*.

'Sure?' He sat tensely on the edge of his seat,

looking down at City Road.

'Sure I'm sure. There's the Steelers' ground, see.' Daisy pointed out the famous stadium lights two streets away. Highfield had been the city's home ground for more than fifty years; a meeting place for football fans everywhere.

Jimmy saw the ground and fell quiet. Perhaps he was dreaming of the goal he would score for the Steelers at Highfield one day. *His power-packed right foot would pile the ball into the back of the net and the League title would be theirs . . .*

Meanwhile, the bus shuddered to a halt to let on more passengers.

Daisy glanced down and recognised a familiar, untidy figure in the queue. 'Oh no!' she groaned. How unlucky could you be when you set out to run away? First Winona, now Nathan!

There was no mistaking Nathan Moss. There was only one boy in the world whose faded fair hair stuck out at weird angles like that, whose glasses were always mended by tape, and whose shoelaces were always undone . . .

'Hey, Jimmy. Hey, Daisy,' Nathan muttered as he climbed the stairs. He sat down in the seat behind them, dumping the trumpet case he was carrying on the floor between his feet. Then he got out a small plastic wallet and carefully slid his yellow bus ticket into one of the

slots, alongside a pink one, a blue one and a boring beige one.

'I collect them,' he explained to Daisy. 'Every time I go to Music Centre for my trumpet lesson, I use a new route so I can buy a different colour ticket.'

Like, *wow*! she thought. But at least Nathan was too weird to wonder what she and Jimmy were up to. She hoped.

'How's Legs?' she asked, to divert attention from the bulky rucksack beside her.

'Legs is fine,' Nathan replied. Then, 'What have you got in that bag?'

'Dirty washing,' Daisy said, quick as a flash. 'Our

washing machine broke down, so I have to take it to the laundrette.'

'Hmm.' Nathan spotted Jimmy's similar bag. 'How about you?'

'Same thing.' Jimmy coloured up straight away.

He was a terrible liar, Daisy knew. And he didn't seem to be happy with the way their running-away plan was working out. In fact, she'd never known Jimmy to be so quiet and stiff; most unlike his usual self.

Nathan frowned. 'Don't you think that's a really interesting coincidence?' he said. 'Seeing as you two live next door to one another and both your washing machines have broken down at the same time?'

Was he joking? Daisy stared hard at Nathan's pale face and electric-shock hair. Nope, he seemed deadly serious. He really *was* deep into working out the chances of two Zanussis on the same street breaking down together.

'Sorry, Nathan, this is our stop!' Jumping up from the seat, Daisy dragged Jimmy down the aisle.

Slowly Nathan turned his head. 'Hey, Daisy!' he called, glasses glinting in the sunlight. 'I expect you don't want me to mention that I saw you?'

'Yeah . . . I mean, no . . . I mean, yeah, don't say anything!' she stammered.

She jumped off the bus ahead of Jimmy, then

glanced up to see Nathan still staring gleefully down at them from his high seat. And she could have sworn he winked.

'Is it that obvious?' Daisy muttered, striding through a crowd of pigeons pecking grain in Fountain Square. 'I mean, do we look like two kids who are running away from home?'

Jimmy ran to keep up. 'Yeah,' he told her. 'We do.'

Pigeons flapped and flew off in all directions as Daisy and Jimmy charged through their midst.

'Hey you!' an old man with a bag of pigeon-food yelled. 'Walk, don't run!' The fat grey birds wheeled overhead and swooped down again. *Peck-peck-peck* at the food, *waddle-waddle* towards the man in the old shell-suit.

Jimmy and Daisy slowed down. They came to a halt by the steps to the Central Library.

'What are we looking for?' Jimmy asked.

'The Information Office, to ask about the Academy,' she reminded him.

'Don't just stand there!' A woman pushing twins in a wide pushchair complained that they were blocking her way.

Jimmy and Daisy scuttled clear. Then Jimmy spotted a blue sign with a white 'i', plus an arrow pointing across the square. 'Over there!' he cried.

He led the charge back through the flock of over-fed pigeons, up on to the low wall surrounding the tall fountain, along the brim, getting splashed to bits. 'Yeah!' he yelled wildly as the icy water spattered down.

'I'm wet through!' Daisy cried. Hair, T-shirt, rucksack; everything.

'Get down from that wall, you two!' a man in a bright yellow plastic jacket cried; a council worker employed to clean up the square after the pigeons.

Miserable spoilsport! Daisy groaned and jumped down, squelching after Jimmy, who always seemed to run faster, balance better, kick the ball further than anyone else she knew.

They arrived at the Information Office out of breath and dripping wet.

'Close that door!' The woman behind the desk looked up as soon as they walked in. She was as grey and over-fed as the pigeons, with her dull hair frizzed out in a perm. 'And don't slop water over my nice clean floor!'

Don't – don't – don't! It seemed to Daisy that she could never escape that dreaded word.

The Information Officer carried on glaring at her two new customers. 'Stay there. Don't move until you've drip-dried!' she instructed.

Jimmy stood by the door in his wet football strip, his teeth chattering, knobbly knees knocking. He stared around at the rows of maps and leaflets, the posters on the walls, the shiny souvenirs on the counter. 'P-p-please . . .' he began.

'Wait a moment, I'm busy!' the woman snapped, disappearing from behind her desk into a back room.

Daisy pulled a face. All they wanted to do was ask a simple question.

So they waited. And dripped. And waited.

Outside, the sunlight reached the fountain and lit up a million sparkling drops. More people crossed the square with shopping bags, pushing bicycles and pushchairs. A man with a guitar and a thin brown dog set out a collection box and began to play.

The fat grey woman peered out from her inner room. 'Still here?' she snapped at Jimmy and Daisy before she vanished again.

In the warmth of the sun Daisy felt her T-shirt begin to steam. It was time to wander across to one of the racks of leaflets, flick through, and try to find one about the Kevin Crowe Academy.

So she and Jimmy shuffled towards the sports and leisure section. They spotted a leaflet for the steam railway, the swimming-pool, the ice-skating rink, but nothing for the new soccer school.

'Don't mess up my display!' Mizz Frizz returned to catch them fingering the leaflets in her precious rack.

Jimmy and Daisy cowered back. Then Daisy gathered her courage. She walked firmly towards the desk. 'We'd like some information, please.'

'What *kind* of information?' the woman grumped.

'Sport and leisure. We're looking for a leaflet –'

'I can see that. I'm not blind.'

'– on the new soccer school for under-twelves run by the ex-Steelers goalkeeper, Kevin Crowe,' Daisy gabbled.

'Huh, then you're wasting your time.' The Information Officer sounded pleased that she was unable to help. Her chins wobbled as she shook her head and told them that there was no such leaflet in print.

'How come?' Jimmy asked, a worried look creeping on to his face.

'Because there's no such school.'

'But it was in the paper. We read about it!' Daisy felt a shockwave run through her body. What did she mean, 'no such school'?

'Yeah, Kevin Crowe is running a live-in Soccer Academy for talented youngsters!' Jimmy recalled the newspaper piece word for word. 'We're going to join!'

The chins wobbled, the little beady eyes disappeared behind a fat smile. 'Dream on, sonny!'

'Dream on'? Daisy gripped the edge of the desk. 'What are you saying? Why can't we join the school?'

The woman smiled down at them and delivered the all-important piece of information that Jimmy and Daisy had both missed in the newspaper.

'Because it isn't open yet,' she told them. 'In fact, they haven't even found a building, or got the money to set it up.'

No building? No money? No soccer school to run away to?

Daisy's dream plummeted to the ground like a dead pigeon.

'Come back next year,' the woman suggested. 'And mind you don't drip on my carpet as you leave!'

Five

Daisy pulled a damp Herbie out of her bag and hugged him.

Jimmy stood in Fountain Square holding back the tears. 'What now?' he asked.

Now we'll never clinch the Cup for Steelers. We'll be failures and we'll never be able to go home in triumph . . . All Daisy's hopes were shattered.

'I mean, what-do-we-do-now?' Jimmy gabbled, a look of panic in his eyes.

Buses and trucks roared around the square, the man with the thin dog and the guitar wailed an unhappy song.

'Leavin' on a jet-plane

Don't know when I'll be back again

Oh, babe, I hate to go . . .'

The dog rested his chin on his front paws and whimpered.

Daisy looked up at the fountain, at millions of sparkling water drops, and failed to find an answer to Jimmy's desperate question.

'Do we go home?' he insisted.

Daisy pictured the scene. She would turn up on the doorstep of Pizza Palazzo with an embarrassed grin on her face. Her farewell letter would be open and lying flat on the table. Her mum would cry all over her and ask what she'd done to deserve a daughter like Daisy. Her dad would look disappointed and carry on sprinkling cheese on the pizzas.

'Can't!' she muttered to Jimmy. *Anything but that.*

'Why not?'

'Because . . . !'

OK, so the Kevin Crowe Academy didn't exist. So they couldn't return to Duke Street amidst clouds of footballing glory, but there must be something else they could do.

Jimmy's unhappy frown deepened. His bottom lip quivered.

Chink-chink, the coins dropped into the guitarist's collection box.

'So kiss me and smile for me . . .

Tell me that you'll wait for me . . .'

'Hmm-hmmm-mmm!' the dog whined and pricked up its ears. Then it lifted its head and caught a sudden movement behind the fountain. Two seconds later, it was on its feet and trotting to investigate.

'Hey, leave Legs alone!' a familiar voice cried.

'Nathan!' Jimmy and Daisy sprang into action. They skirted the fountain after the dog and came face to face with Nathan Moss and Winona Jones.

Nathan hastily popped his giant spider back into its jam-jar while Winona shooed the dog away. 'I told you to leave Legs inside his jar!' she said crossly. '*Now* look what happened!'

Nathan shrugged, then spotted an amazed Daisy and Jimmy. He gave them a weird smile. 'Don't blame me. It was her idea.'

'What are you doing here?' Daisy demanded. Couldn't Winona Jones, just for once in her life, leave her alone?

'Following you. It's OK, I asked permission from Miss Ambler. She got somebody else to do the orange juice and biscuits.'

'How about you?' Daisy asked Nathan. 'Why can't you mind your own business?'

'I just bumped into Winona outside Music Centre, and tracking you two down sounded amusing,' he explained, screwing the jam-jar lid down and perching Legs on the concrete rim surrounding the fountain.

'Yeah, hah-hah! Well done. Now that you found us, what are you gonna do?' Daisy stood with her hands on her hips. 'Sneak off and tell Miss Ambler, why don't you? Go on, get us into trouble, and it's not even a school day!'

Winona frowned severely. 'Daisy, it's for your own good. You can't just run away to a soccer school...'

'Which doesn't even exist,' Nathan added swiftly. Trust Nathan to have checked his facts first.

'So, what's it to you?' For the first time Jimmy joined in the argument. He stooped to pat the bothersome dog, who'd come back to join them carrying a chewed tennis ball in its mouth. Jimmy took the ball and chucked it straight into the water for the dog to fetch.

Woof! The thin brown dog jumped into the sparkling fountain, retrieved the scraggy ball and emerged from the water dripping wet.

'Yuck!' Winona screeched as the dog shook itself dry. Her pretty pink shirt and white trousers were drenched.

'Watch it!' Nathan warned. The dog almost knocked Legs' jam-jar from the ledge into the fountain. He scrabbled to catch it, like a cricketer fielding in the slips.

Daisy seized her chance. 'Run!' she yelled at Jimmy. No way were they going to stick around to be turned in by Winona and Nathan. No, the intention was to lose the enemy, then re-group.

So they ran.

Through the fountain, with the mad brown dog plunging after them. Across the square, up the library ramp, sploshing and dripping every step of the way. Through the sliding doors, leaving the dog behind and with no sign of Winona, Nathan or Legs in pursuit.

'This way!' Jimmy cried, running between rows of books.

Up the escalator to the art gallery, down a long, deserted room lined with portraits of women in big, hooped dresses and men in plumed hats on horseback. The gallery attendant woke up from her doze too late to stop Daisy and Jimmy from using the emergency exit.

Then down the stairs, out of the building through a back door into a car park, dodging between parked cars, nipping under a striped barrier, legging it across the road to the safety of the Marshway Shopping Centre.

'Phew!' The flight had sent the blood rushing through Daisy's veins. Her heart thumped hard against her ribs. But now they were inside the glass-covered maze of shops, there was no chance of Winona

and Nathan picking up their trail.

For a start, the place was crowded with Saturday shoppers. OK, so kids stared at Daisy and Jimmy's dripping figures as they sped by McDonalds. So the two of them looked like they were on the run, bumping into people with their bags, glancing over their shoulders every step of the way. But who cared?

They had lost Nathan and Winona. They came out the far side of Marshway with fresh hope.

'You still wanna know what I think we should do now?' Daisy demanded. She pushed her long, black-brown hair out of her eyes and squared her shoulders.

Jimmy nodded eagerly. He stood in front of an electrical goods shop window filled with fifty TV screens all playing an identical sports programme.

Football, football, football.

Teletext news about players who were injured, the

latest mega-bucks transfers, the announcement of a new team coach to lead the Steelers to Premiership victory.

'Turn around and take a look!' Daisy invited him. It was there on the screen; the news that their team had appointed Kevin Crowe to replace Henri Argent, the coach who had left earlier in the week to return to his native France.

Kevin Crowe, all-time great goalie, local hero and now the new trainer at Highfield.

Fifty identical, smiling Kevin Crowes stared down at Daisy and Jimmy from the TV screens. It was like a sign, a secret message telling them what they should do next.

'C'mon!' Daisy said, without spelling it out in full.

'If we move fast, we can reach the ground before Kevin arrives to greet the team!'

'Robbie, over here!'

'Robbie-Robbie-Robbie. Rob-Rob-Rob!'

'Sign this programme for me please, Robbie . . . oh, please!'

A hundred fans mobbed the star player at the players' clubhouse entrance.

Head down, Robbie Exley made his way through the crowd. His blond hair shone like corn stubble in the sunlight and there was a pleased smile on his handsome, square face.

'Jimmy, look who just arrived!' Daisy jabbed her friend with her elbow. 'Go ahead, get his autograph, before he disappears inside!'

But Jimmy was overcome, unable to move a muscle. He stood at the edge of the precious ground, catching a glimpse of his hero through dozens of yelling fans.

So Daisy acted for him.

She squeezed through to the front of the mob, bobbing under arms, sliding through narrow gaps and ending up next to the man himself.

Robbie was grinning as he signed a young fan's autograph book with a fat felt-tip.

'That's it!' he insisted, putting the top back on the pen. 'I'm out of time. Would you let me through?'

Daisy stood in his path, staring up at him. 'My friend Jimmy thinks you're the best soccer player in the world!'

'He does?' Robbie's grin widened. He looked down at a scruffy, determined, dark-haired kid. ('Robbie-Robbie-Robbie. Rob-Rob-Rob!')

She nodded. 'He wants to play like you one day.'

'So I'd better watch my back!' The superstar laughed and sidestepped Daisy.

She ran after him. 'Can he have your autograph?'

Robbie gave in and unscrewed the pen top. 'Where's your autograph book?'

Oh no, no book. Not even a sheet of paper! So Daisy

turned around and offered the back of her pale-blue T-shirt. 'Sign this!' she begged.

Robbie grinned again, then recited the words which he scrawled. 'To Jimmy – with best wishes to a star of the future. Yours, Robbie Exley.'

'Magic!' Jimmy whispered. He read the message on the back of Daisy's T-shirt.

'It's yours, Jimmy!' she promised. 'As soon as I get back home – no, as soon as I find something else to wear – you can have this T-shirt for keeps!'

Jimmy's eyes shone, a smile lit up his pointed,

flushed face. It was like he'd died and gone to heaven. 'Thanks, Daisy!'

'Watch out, you two!' a fellow fan warned, as a swish silver car cruised towards the entrance.

Daisy and Jimmy squashed against the gate-post. They watched the passenger door swing open and the Steelers' new coach, Kevin Crowe, step out.

Kevin was dressed in a smart suit, blue shirt and dark blue tie with a Steelers' logo. His grey hair was cut short, his lean face tanned. He smiled and waved a hand as the cheers and good-luck calls of the gathered fans rang out.

Someone opened the players' entrance door from the inside. 'The boss is a busy man. Let him through,' a voice ordered. But Daisy was flushed with her Robbie Exley success and she had no intention of missing this chance.

She and Jimmy were small. The door was wide, and an unruly bunch of autograph-hunters almost knocked down the doorman. So Daisy and Jimmy ducked to crawl between a few pairs of legs. Before they knew it, they were through the gate with their unwitting soccer hero.

Daisy was close enough to reach out and touch him. But was she brave enough to ask him the only question that mattered to her in the whole world?

Six

'Can Jimmy Black and me be your first pupils at the Under-Twelves' Soccer Academy?'

This was Daisy's fall-back plan, formed on the hoof as she and Jimmy ran away from nosey-parkers Winona and Nathan. She'd seen the item about Kevin Crowe's new job on the TV sport round-up, and decided there and then to put their names at the very top of the list. Once Kevin had accepted them as his first full-time pupils, all she and Jimmy had to do was stay in hiding for a year until the Academy opened its doors.

'How do we hide for a whole year?' Jimmy had asked.

'Easy.' Firmly dismissing his doubts, Daisy had described how they would find a boarded-up flat near the football ground and become squatters. They would live there in secret.

'Are we old enough?'

'Jimmy!' She'd sighed and rolled her eyes. 'Do you want to do this, or not?'

He'd swallowed, nodded and tagged along. 'But what do we eat?' he'd wanted to know.

'Stuff,' Daisy had said. Like, *Don't bother me with small details*. Then, 'We can get paper-rounds to earn some money and buy Big Macs.' Easy.

'Are we old enough?' Doggedly Jimmy pointed out the problems.

'We can pretend to be twelve, can't we?'

'OK, so how do we keep warm in winter? Do we tell our families where we are so they can lend us a heater?'

Daisy had despaired of answering his questions. 'Trust me,' she'd pleaded. 'All we have to do is speak to Kevin outside the players' entrance. After that, all the rest will fall into place!'

And here they were now. The doorman was still battling to shut the gate on the noisy fans, and the Greatest Goalkeeper of All Time was considering their request.

'Let me get this straight. You've sneaked in here after me in order to enrol in the junior soccer school when it opens?'

Daisy and Jimmy both nodded until their heads nearly fell off. 'We could be your very first signings,' Daisy pleaded. 'Jimmy's ace with his right foot, and I'm pretty good with my left.'

The corners of Kevin's mouth twitched. 'I admire your cheek,' he told them. Then he ordered the cross-looking doorman not to bother trying to eject the intruders. 'I've got five minutes to spare before I give the lads their team-talk, so why don't you two come along with me to inspect the pitch?'

'Honest?' Jimmy gaped, going weak at the knees.

'Sure, if you're quick.' Kevin led the way into the clubhouse, past the players' changing-rooms, down a corridor and out through the tunnel on to the smoothest stretch of grass Daisy and Jimmy had ever seen.

The turf which rolled out before them was clipped and trimmed and rolled. It was marked out with straight, pure white lines and the pitch was empty except for the ground staff who positioned corner flags and checked the nets.

'Hey, boss,' a man in a yellow tracksuit said as he jogged by, carrying a string-bag bulging with footballs.

'Nice to have you back, boss,' another said, dashing

into the clubhouse with a stack of programmes.

'Nice to be back, Charlie.' Kevin greeted them and strolled on ahead of Daisy and Jimmy. He tested the turf with the toe of his shoe, then gazed around the ground at the banks of empty terraces.

In the magic of the moment, Daisy pictured them full. Each stand bursting at the seams with cheering, chanting fans.

'Jimm-mmy Black, Jimm-mmy Black!' Then, 'Dais-ee, Dais-ee, give them their answer, do!' They roared out the old song with special small changes: 'We're half-crazy, all for the love of you!'

Daisy accepted their cheers. She limbered up under dazzling lights, shook hands with the opposition, took up her position in the centre of the pitch. Jimmy was on the right wing, hungry for the ball as usual. The whistle blew. The cup tie had begun . . .

'What do you say to a short trial right here and now?' good-natured Kevin Crowe invited. He took a ball from one of his staff and rolled it across the grass towards Jimmy.

'Honest?' he gasped again in disbelief. 'Here? Now?'

'Pass to me, Jim!' Daisy cut in eagerly. She jogged on the spot to loosen up, put in a short sprint towards the centre line, then waited for him to tap the ball.

'Dais-ee! Dais-ee!' Sixty thousand people roared her name.

Jimmy overcame his nerves to produce a smart, accurate pass.

Daisy took the ball and ran with it. She swerved around an imaginary defender, then flicked the ball back to Jimmy.

'Steel-ers, Steel-ers, Steel-ers!' Passing back and forth, Jimmy and Daisy dribbled the full length of the pitch, encouraged by Kevin Crowe, who ran with them until they reached the goalmouth. Then he took up his old position as keeper, crouching low, ready to deflect any shot that flew towards him.

'Offside!' a mob of angry opposition fans protested as Daisy made the final, unselfish pass. 'Referee!'

'No way was that offside!' Daisy muttered under her breath. 'Go for it, Jimmy; shoot!'

Jimmy swung back his left foot, then booted the ball at the goal. It skimmed the ground like a bullet, slipping under the great Kevin Crowe's grasp and thudding into the back of the net.

'Ye-e-e-es!' The Steelers' fans went mad with delight.

Jimmy leaped in the air, then did three forward flips. Daisy ran to embrace him and share the applause.

'Not bad!' Kevin grinned. He stooped to fish the ball out of the back corner. 'Who taught you two to play soccer?'

'Nobody,' Jimmy muttered. 'We just learned in the park.'

'Well, consider your names at the top of the list for the Academy when it opens,' Kevin promised them, glancing at his watch and seeing that he'd run short of time. 'I'm hoping to hold a two-week summer school in July next year, as long as I get the go-ahead from the board of governors to use the Steelers' training ground.'

'Two weeks?' Daisy came down to earth with a bump.

'Yes, that's the plan.' The coach walked them back towards the tunnel. 'We'll be offering fifty places for a fortnight's live-in course during the long holidays.'

'So we'd have to go back to school afterwards?' Jimmy double-checked. Bad news. In fact, major disaster, as far as Daisy's grand running-away plan went.

'Sorry about that.' Kevin laughed at their shocked faces. Then he turned to one side to take out his mobile phone and answer a loud ring. 'Yes, this is Kevin Crowe,' he said, then listened. 'Could you repeat those two names? . . . Right, yes, I see. Got that!'

Clicking the off-button, he looked closely at Jimmy and Daisy. 'How about you two joining me in five minutes in the executive suite to talk over your future plans?' he invited.

'Can you believe this?' Jimmy hissed.

They'd got over the shock of learning that their stay at the soccer academy was going to be a short one and decided that they could change their running-away plan to suit the new situation. In any case, they had to concentrate on the moment in hand.

He and Daisy were surrounded by silver trophies and shields. They lined the walls of the posh suite, alongside photographs of the Steelers going back forty or fifty years.

Wall-to-wall carpet woven in the Steelers' own special two-tone stripes. Squeaky leather armchairs and low glass tables. A wide window with a perfect view of the pitch below.

'Do I believe this? No; pinch me to see if I'm awake!' she whispered back. 'Ouch, not that hard!'

'Sorry – not!' Jimmy trotted around the room, heading an imaginary ball. He gave a victory salute to the winners of the 1953 FA Cup Final.

'Kevin Crowe wants to discuss our futures!' Daisy needed to say it out loud, over and over. She checked the clock on the wall. 'He'll meet us here after he's delivered his team talk, which will be in one minute and twenty seconds precisely! How brilliant is that?'

'Yeah!' Jimmy sighed. 'You know all that stuff he

said about working hard at our ball skills and not giving in until we get where we want to be?'

Daisy nodded, one eye on the ticking clock, one eye on the door through which the Great Man would return. 'He was right. And I quote: "Talent alone is never enough. It's the dedication that counts."'

'I'm one hundred per cent dedicated!' Jimmy swore.

'Me too. Football is my life. Isn't it cool?'

They sighed and each sank into a leather armchair with a squeak and a hiss of air. Then they sat up again as they heard footsteps come up the stairs. Not just one set, but two or three. It sounded to them like Kevin was returning with perhaps a couple of members of

the team to add their encouragement. Maybe even Robbie Exley himself!

They braced themselves as the door opened.

And there, framed by cups and medals, stood Miss Ambler, flanked by Winona Jones and Nathan Moss.

Seven

How? What? When? Where?

How had it all gone so horribly wrong?

What would happen now?

When had Winona and Nathan put two and two together to guess where Jimmy and Daisy had run off to?

Where were the runaways' dreams of glory now?

Burst like a bubble, that's where. Vanished with a small pop into thin air.

'Don't look so downcast.' Miss Ambler spoke kindly as she advanced towards them. Behind her, Nathan looked wise and serious, while even Winona managed not to smile smugly.

'B-b-but!' was all Jimmy could manage to whisper.

Daisy felt the walls of the Steelers' executive suite tilt and spin. She had to grab on to Jimmy for support.

Miss Rambler-Ambler came towards them offering smiles and sympathy. 'Never mind,' she comforted. 'No one's going to be angry with you for running away. Let's just talk about it, shall we, and try to sort things out.'

No, please! For one awful moment Daisy imagined the teacher putting her arms around her and giving her the sugary hug treatment. Personally, she preferred the 'Daisy, don't do that!' and 'You're a complete disgrace!' approach.

'Miss, we never ran away!' Jimmy claimed, bravely stepping between Miss Ambler and Daisy. 'What gave you that idea?'

Great thinking, Jim! 'Yeah, Miss, who said anything about running away?' Daisy piped up.

Miss Ambler faltered and took half a pace back. 'Winona?' she said, with a puzzled glance over her shoulder.

'Please, Miss, I heard them planning it outside the playground.' Winona looked worried.

'Ttt-ttt!' Daisy said. 'You heard us mention the Kevin Crowe Academy, fair enough,' she admitted. 'But what gave you the idea that we needed to *run away* to join it?'

'Yeah!' Jimmy was in full flow. He frowned and looked daggers at Nathan. 'Everyone knows you only join up for two weeks during the summer holidays. You don't live there for ever!'

Wow, had Jimmy suddenly got good at lying! Daisy felt really proud of him.

Miss Ambler fell for it completely. 'You mean, it's all been a mistake? There was no need for any of this big drama after all?'

Daisy smiled as Winona and Nathan shuffled their feet and coughed uncomfortably. Talk about being wrong-footed and caught in the offside trap!

'Everything sorted?' Kevin Crowe popped his head around the door to check things out. Changed into his tracksuit, he was on his way to take up his position on the pitch, ready for the start of the afternoon's training session.

'Yes, fine thanks!' the teacher said quickly. 'In fact, Mr Crowe, we're sorry to have bothered you with that emergency phone call. It seems that Winona and Nathan may have over-reacted to the situation somewhat in thinking we had a huge crisis on our hands. All that Daisy and Jimmy had in mind was to speak to you about enrolling in the Academy; nothing else.'

Kevin nodded and winked. 'Good. No problem then.' He beckoned Daisy to the door and held out two small white pieces of paper. 'Tickets for next week's Cup match,' he explained. 'Directors' box. See you there.'

Daisy took the tickets and stammered her thanks.

'And remember, all being well, you're top of the list for the soccer academy next summer!'

Jimmy's skinny frame swelled with pride and pleasure.

Yes! Daisy thought. *Yes! Yes! Yes!*

Then Miss Ambler shepherded them out of the clubhouse, through eager fans hanging hopefully around the gate, to her rusty orange VW Beetle.

Daisy, Jimmy, Nathan and Winona squeezed in and the teacher drove them back to school.

Next to Miss Ambler in the front passenger seat, Nathan let Legs out of his jar and stroked him thoughtfully.

Squashed between Daisy and Jimmy on the back seat, Winona was NOT happy. 'You don't know the full story yet!' she hissed.

But Daisy just waved her cup ticket in Winona's face, then squirmed around to show off Robbie Exley's autograph on the back of her T-shirt.

'And remember, Winona,' Miss Ambler said sternly as she unloaded them outside the school gates. 'Check your facts before you raise the alarm. If we'd called in

the police and informed Daisy and Jimmy's parents, we'd have caused a terrific amount of fuss and worry over nothing!'

'Yes, Miss.' Winona clasped her hands in front of her and bowed her head. It seemed she had more to say, but for the moment had decided against it.

So the final score was definitely one-nil to Jimmy and Daisy.

* * *

That is, until they had left school well behind them and were on their way back home to Duke Street.

Daisy's bag bumped against her shoulder, Jimmy trotted along beside her.

Miss Ambler's last words were echoing inside her head.

'If we'd called in the police and alerted Daisy and Jimmy's parents, we'd have caused a terrific amount of fuss and worry over nothing.'

'Mum and Dad!' she gasped, stopping dead on the pavement.

It was the middle of the afternoon. Her dramatic farewell note had been sitting in front of the microwave at home for seven whole hours!

Disaster!

'My note!' she moaned to her co-plotter, Jimmy. 'They'll have picked it up and read it. Now we're gonna be in real trouble!'

Daisy Morelli, go to your room! What did we do to deserve this? Why can't you be more like Winona Jones?

'You mean, **you're** gonna be in real trouble!' Jimmy reminded Daisy that **he** hadn't left a note. He got ready his own excuses and slipped away.

'Thanks a lot!' Deserted, Daisy unwillingly opened the door to her place.

'Daisy *mia*!' her dad cried, all smiles from behind the counter of the restaurant. His red striped apron was covered in white flour, his face flushed from the heat of the ovens.

'You enjoy yourself with your friend, Winona, huh? You eat a good lunch at her place?'

My friend Winona? Lunch at her place? What was this?

'Daisy, look at the mess you're in as usual!' Angie Morelli squeezed between the busy tables, carrying baby Mia on one hip. She hustled Daisy into the back kitchen and sat her down. 'And next time, don't go off without telling me where you're going!' she warned. 'It's only thanks to Winona that we knew what you were up to.'

'How come?' Daisy asked weakly. What was going on? Why weren't her mum and dad crazy with worry after reading her note? What did Winona have to do with anything?

'Well, she was the one who had the sense to pop in here and let us know where you were. I hope you thanked Mrs Jones for giving you lunch and looking after you.'

Her mind still in chaos, Daisy snuck a glance at the microwave. No note.

'Winona also picked up the birthday card for Nathan that you'd forgotten to take with you,' Angie explained calmly, following the direction of Daisy's worried look. 'That was nice of her, wasn't it?'

Daisy mumbled and nodded. *Now* she got it; not only had Winona guessed Jimmy and Daisy's every move, she'd also covered for them at home so as not to worry their parents. She'd even whisked away the tell-tale letter and carried out the whole cover-up perfectly.

Groaning, Daisy sagged forward in her chair. It seemed she owed Winona-Perfecta-Jones more than she could ever repay.

Rats! Rats! Rats!

'Daisy, what on earth . . . ?' Angie Morelli spotted the felt-tip message scrawled on the back of her daughter's T-shirt and read it out loud. '"To Jimmy – with best wishes to a star of the future. Yours, Robbie Exley"!'

As Daisy jumped to her feet and backed against the wall, she dropped her bag. Out fell her toothbrush and a soggy Herbie.

'Daisy?' Her mum stooped to pick up the hamster. 'I thought you'd left him in your school drawer . . . ?'

Think fast. Dream up a good excuse.

'Well?' her mum asked.

Fat baby Mia goo-gooed and chortled on her hip. In her chubby fist she held a chewed photo of her big sister, Daisy.

'Well . . .' Daisy began.

She didn't get any further. Her mum marched up to her and turned her around, re-read the message on her back and immediately ordered her upstairs. 'Take that T-shirt off and put it straight in the washing-machine!' she ordered.

'B-b-but . . . I can't . . . It's for Jimmy . . . it could be worth a fortune!'

'Daisy!' Angie insisted. The tune never changed, it was always exactly the same. 'YOU' *(push up the stairs)* 'ARE' *(march through the bedroom door)* 'A' *(stern stare, hands on hips)* 'DISGRACE!!!'

Just you wait, Winona!

Jenny Oldfield

Illustrated by
Lauren Child

One

'And Daisy Morelli is going for the World Handstand Record!'

Leonie Flowers used her fist as a microphone. She commentated on Daisy's attempt to cross the playground on her hands.

'Yes, she's pacing herself perfectly, going strongly down the final stretch . . . !' Leonie's voice rose with excitement.

'Watch out, Nathan!' Jimmy Black cleared Daisy's path, getting all the kids to shoo out of her way.

Daisy felt the blood rush to her head so that her eyes practically popped out of their sockets. Her wrists ached, her arms shook, but she gritted her teeth and walked bravely on.

'And now she only has ten metres to go!' Leonie gabbled, reaching fever-pitch. 'Will she make it . . . ? (Get off the official World Record Track, Winona!) This magnificent athlete is staggering a little as the effort begins to tell . . .

'But if Morelli succeeds in this attempt, it'll go down in the history of sport as one of mankind's greatest achievements...!'

Daisy's legs swayed and wobbled in mid-air. She saw everything upside-down: the playground wall, kids' feet and legs, Winona Jones's neat, black patent leather shoes.

'Daisy, stop that at once. You'll do yourself an injury!'

Winona doubled forward so that her blonde curly hair and smooth pink face appeared in Daisy's line of vision.

'Get-out-of-my-way!' Daisy grunted. Eight metres, seven metres, six metres to go. Would her arms last out?

Winona was still there. 'The blood will all rush to your head . . . you'll get blisters on your hands . . . Daisy Morelli, I can see your belly-button!'

Grunt-grunt. Five metres to go. Daisy's legs felt as heavy as lead. But the whole of Woodbridge Junior was watching this attempt and she refused to give in.

Dong-dong-dong! Daisy heard something that sounded like a playground bell explode inside her head. Oh no; she'd had a brain seizure from being

upside down for too long. She'd overdone it, like Winona warned. This was it . . . the end! She sagged and sank to the ground.

'Aah!' Maya, Kyle, Jared and Jade sighed as the record attempt failed. 'Nearly! Yeah, that's a shame. Pity Winona had to go and ring the stupid bell!'

Finding her brain still in one piece inside her skull and her blood still pumping normally, Daisy opened her eyes.

And there was Winona-Stupid-Jones standing over her, playground bell in hand, saying with a smirky-smile, 'Oh, sorry, Daisy. Did I make you jump?'

* * *

'Have you seen your hair lately?' Winona asked, standing in front of Daisy later that morning in the queue for the school photographer.

Daisy ignored her. After what Winona had done during her world record attempt, she had sworn in public, surrounded by Jimmy and the rest of the gang, never to speak to Winona again.

'Your hair's a complete mess,' Winona advised, overlooking the fact that Daisy had ignored her. 'Here, would you like to borrow my brush?'

Winona's own blonde curls were in perfect order.

The queue shuffled forward as Maya took her place in front of the camera and smiled shyly into the lens.

'Just you wait, Winona!' Daisy muttered under her breath, forgetting her earlier oath. She glared at the hairbrush, then deliberately mussed up her long, dark hair some more.

'You've got felt-tip marks all down the front of your shirt,' Winona pointed out primly, dipping into her pocket and offering Daisy her spare school tie to cover up the mess.

I'd like to strangle you with that! Daisy thought darkly.

Jimmy's turn to face the camera had arrived. Daisy watched her best friend try to push his floppy brown hair back from his forehead in a failed attempt to tidy himself up. Then he stepped forward like a soldier in front of the firing-squad, chin jutting, teeth clenched.

'Say sausages!' the photographer ordered.

'Sausages!' Jimmy flinched as the camera clicked.

'Next!'

And Leonie took Jimmy's place, laid back as always, her black curly hair in a neat halo around her face, a wide smile and big, shiny brown eyes.

'Say sausages!'

'Saus-age-'(*click*)'-s.'

'Good. Next!' The busy photographer kept the kids coming.

It was Nathan Moss's turn. He took his place, complete with Legs, his pet spider.

Legs perched on Nathan's shoulder, happy to have his photograph taken.

The man behind the camera focused. 'Say saus... Good Lord, what on earth's that?' He sprang back to a safe distance, staring in horror at Nathan's fat black pet.

'This is Legs,' Nathan said, matter-of-factly. 'He's perfectly harmless.'

To prove the point, Legs stretched each of his eight legs and took a stroll around the back of Nathan's neck, to reappear confidently on the other shoulder.

'Sweet!' Leonie whispered brightly as she passed by Daisy and Winona still waiting in the queue. They were all used to weird Nathan and his unusual pet.

But she happened to catch Winona making an attack with her hairbrush on an unwilling Daisy's tangled hair. And Leonie shot Daisy a puzzled look, running to catch up with Jimmy and whisper in a loud voice, 'Since when did Daisy make friends with Winona Jones?'

Jimmy shrugged and glanced back at the two girls in the queue.

'I didn't!' Daisy hissed hotly. She wished with all her heart that she could get Miss Perfect out of her hair. Literally.

But Jimmy and Leonie didn't hear. First a failed record attempt, now this. Daisy knew that her reputation had hit an all-time low.

'Daisy Morelli, she ees, 'ow you say, ze traitor!' Standing daydreaming in the photographer's queue, Daisy pictured a dark underground tunnel; probably a sewer under the streets of Paris. Jimmy and Leonie were resistance fighters during the Second World War, which they'd just finished watching a video about in history.

'Nev-aire!' Jimmy's face went pale with shock. 'Thees Daisy, she is our number one agent. 'Ow can she be ze enemy?'

The black sewer dripped and gurgled as Leonie convinced Jimmy that Daisy, their leader, had indeed changed sides.

'. . . It's a lie!' Daisy declared when Jimmy and Leonie finally cornered her in a slimy, rotting corner of the sewers and faced her, pistols in hand. 'I swear I never wanted to even speak to Winona Jones, never mind let her comb my hair!'

Leonie and Jimmy had refused to listen . . .

'Next!' the photographer barked from his position behind the camera.

The portrait-taker had dealt hastily with Nathan and Legs, then moved on to Winona.

Winona stepped into position with a well-rehearsed smile. Her tie was neatly knotted, her white collar spotless.

'Sausages!' she said without prompting.

Click. 'Perfect! Next!'

Daisy sat down in front of the lens in a foul mood. Her street-cred was nil, thanks to Winona, who, besides ruining her reputation with Jimmy, Leonie and the rest, had spoiled her best chance yet of winning the handstand record.

So she scowled at Winona's neat rear-view, wondering how on earth she could get her own back.

'Say —' the photographer began.

'Sausages!' Daisy snarled, all teeth and spit. And when Miss Ambler handed over the photos to take home at the end of the day, all Daisy's friends laughed at hers.

Daisy blushed then scowled at her image. No way would her mum and dad want to buy this snarling, snapping portrait.

'You look like a mad dog with rabies,' Winona giggled from her seat next to Daisy. Her own photograph had turned out chocolate-box perfect, of course.

Daisy shoved the horrid picture into her bag, alongside Herbie, her beanie-babe hamster. She pretended not to care, even when Winona insisted on tagging along with her to coo-coo over Daisy's baby sister, Mia, at the school gate.

But inside, she was boiling, fuming, furious. Smoke was coming out of her ears, she was plotting horrible accidents for Winona by fire, flood and earthquake.

'Goo-goo!' Winona stooped to play with Mia's pink rabbit.

'See you tomorrow, Jimmy!' Daisy called out as he passed by with the usual gang – Leonie, Maya, Jared and co.

Her best mate hardly bothered to reply. Instead, Jared passed a secret remark and they all laughed like crazy.

Standing next to Winona, Mia and her mum, Daisy felt snubbed, cut out, cold-shouldered and alone.

'Choo-choo-chobble!' the blonde super-pupil gurgled beside her.

'Goo-goo-ca-choo!' Mia burbled back. In her mind, Daisy was tossing up Winona's savage fate.

She forced the glamorous blonde enemy to the rim of an active volcano. Molten lava smoked and bubbled redly only feet below. Within seconds Winona Jones would be no more . . .

Two

'Rain, rain, rain!' Daisy's dad punched and thumped pizza-dough on a floury board.

Outside the Pizza Palazzo on a typical English Saturday in June the raindrops bounced off the pavement.

'They call this summer!' Gianni gave a rich, deep laugh. 'But here in England there is no sun, no one is smiling. Only rain!'

Daisy stood nearby in a red striped apron, waiting for her dad to hand her a chunk of dough. The smell of cooking pizzas wafted around the restaurant and out on to Duke Street.

'Hey, Daisy, what are you doing here?' Angie Morelli emerged from the wine cellar in the basement. 'How come you're not off playing with the gang?'

''Cos no one bothered to call for me, that's why not.'

Daisy's black mood of the day before had deepened. When Gianni tossed her a fistful of bendy dough, she slapped it on to the board and battered it flat. *Die, die*!

'Hey, you want to kill this pizza or cook it?' her dad protested, slapping his own chunk of dough lightly and niftily between his broad palms.

'So where's Jimmy today?' Angie asked, stacking bottles into the wine rack. Soon the restaurant would be crowded with hungry weekend shoppers wanting lunch.

'Dunno,' Daisy muttered. Don't care.

'And Leonie?'

'Dunno.' *Hammer-hammer-bash.*

'Hmm.' Her mum was just beginning to feel sorry for her when she saw a figure with a red umbrella struggle through the doorway. 'Ah, never mind,' she said brightly. 'Here comes Winona to keep you company!'

No, please, no! Daisy bashed her dough so hard that she made a hole right through the middle. Her dad picked up the sorry grey object between his thumb and forefinger and tutted in dismay. 'Daisy mia, in

Italy they put you in prison for making pizza this way!'

'Hi everyone!' Winona chirped. She shook her wet umbrella then snapped it shut. 'Mrs Morelli, I just happened to be passing and I wondered if you'd like me to look after Mia for a while.'

'How nice!' Angie smiled gratefully. 'Thanks, Winona, but Mia's having her morning nap right now.'

'So come help make pizzas,' Gianni invited. He unhooked a spare apron and showed Winona what to do.

Soon Ms TV Cook of the Year was flipping and twizzling dough like a pro.

'Excellent!' Gianni beamed. 'You want a job making pizza, Winona; you come to Pizza Palazzo any time!'

Winona smiled and blushed modestly at her success.

Sidelined in her own family kitchen, Daisy glared. She was halfway through trying a second time with a fresh piece of dough, making the same sulky botch as before, when the door opened again.

'Hi, Mr Morelli, Hi, Mrs Morelli!' Jimmy piped. He came in carrying his football as always, and wearing his blue-and-white football strip. He hadn't spotted Daisy and Winona working behind the counter.

Leonie and Jared burst in after him. 'We came to see if Daisy wants to play footie . . .' Leonie tailed off when she caught sight of the two busy cooks.

Daisy was doing her best to vanish. Her face was splodged with flour, her fingers sticky with pizza-dough. She even had clumps of it in her hair.

Winona didn't have a stray speck of flour anywhere. 'Hi, everyone!' she chirped. 'It's raining, in case you hadn't noticed!'

'So?' Leonie frowned. She looked suspiciously from Winona to Daisy, then back again.

Winona was nine-going-on-ninety. 'So the park will be muddy. You can hardly play football when the weather's like this!'

'Caught red-handed!' That evening, Daisy consoled herself by confiding in Herbie.

The one-eyed beanie-babe hamster listened quietly. He lay squidged on her duvet, thinking things through.

'I mean, how unlucky can you be!' Daisy went back through the day. 'There I am, innocently helping Dad when Winona shows up. I never asked her, did I? I can't help it if she barges into my life, can I?'

Herbie considered the problem carefully.

'The thing is, Herbie, it looks bad. Jimmy and Leonie think I've made friends with the teacher's pet on purpose. Like, yeah!' She spread her hands, palms upwards. 'Me, Daisy Disaster-Morelli make friends with Winona-Perfecta Jones!

'Crazy, huh?'

'Daisy, stop talking to yourself and go to sleep!' Angie put her head around the door. 'It's half-past ten!'

Daisy waited until her mum closed the door and went away. 'So anyway, I'm meant to be the leader of the gang. Well, not the leader exactly, but I'm the one with good ideas usually.

'Like, Herb, you remember the trouble I went to when Miss Ambler confiscated you that time I took you into assembly?

'It was *my* idea to get Leonie to ask to look in the teacher's locked cupboard for her so-called missing pencil-case. Then Maya had to deliberately spill orange juice all over Roald Dahl to drag Miss Boring-Snoring away so that I could sneak up and grab you

out of the cupboard when she wasn't looking. . . .'
Daisy paused for breath, while Herbie looked faintly bored.

'*Sleep,* Daisy!' Angie was passing along the landing again and heard the chuntering still going on inside Daisy's room.

Daisy sighed and fidgeted under her bedclothes. 'Anyway, the point is, Winona's gone and ruined all that by hanging around me when I don't even ask her. She sticks like glue and I can't bear it. I mean, when I saw Jimmy coming out of his place at teatime, he never even stopped to ask me if I wanted to play footie! Think about it!'

She was so upset at the memory that she didn't notice when her beanie hamster slid down the duvet and over the edge of the bed. He landed with a soft thud on the floor.

'So what am I gonna do?' Daisy whined. 'I mean, Herbie, what would you do in my situation? . . .Herbie? . . . Herb?'

Silence from the hamster.

'Oh great!' she muttered. 'Now even my own hamster is refusing to talk to me!'

Sunday was sunny. Ideal park weather. And no one called.

All during breakfast Daisy waited for Jimmy to

show. She punctured the soft yolk of her poached egg and mopped up every last drop with fingers of toast, kidding herself that it was still early, that soon Jimmy's knock would come and he'd be standing there in his blue-and-white kit, asking her to play.

'Why are you moping around in the house on a lovely sunny morning?' her mum asked, whisking away Daisy's plate and glass.

'I don't feel like going out,' Daisy grunted, twiddling a strand of hair and staring gloomily out of the window.

'In that case, why don't you entertain Mia for half an hour while I pop out for a newspaper?' Angie suggested.

Daisy jumped up from the table, stuck her feet into her trainers and shot out of the door. 'Sorry, Mum. I just remembered I said I'd meet Maya . . .'

Zoom! She was downstairs and out of the door before her mum drew breath.

And now that she was out on the sunny street, she felt more like her usual self.

There were walls to walk along, puddles from yesterday to jump in or over, red men to stop at crossings for and green men to go.

And there was the pet-shop window to stare in, baby rabbits to coo over, a parrot on a stick outside the door to talk to.

'Where's Molly?' the yellow-and-white bird croaked. 'Molly, Molly, Molly! She's my girl!'

Daisy jumped back, then grinned. 'He-llo!' she croaked back in what she thought was a parrot-voice.

'Where's Molly?' The parrot ducked its head then twitched it from side to side. It spread its bright yellow comb of feathers until they stuck up punk-style on top of its head.

'He-llo!' Daisy cooed.

'Molly, Molly, Molly! She's my girl!'

'That's a great conversation you're having there!' Leonie Flowers happened to be passing by, on her way to the park.

Daisy dropped her new friend the parrot and seized her chance to join Leonie. 'Hey,' she said casually.

'Hey,' Leonie replied. She allowed Daisy to walk down the street with her, half-pretending that she wasn't there.

'He-llo!' the parrot called after them.

Daisy and Leonie paused, then grinned over the bird's bad timing.

'So, you coming to play footie?' Leonie wanted to know.

Daisy beamed with relief. Despite the Winona disaster, things in the gang were OK after all. 'Who gets to choose teams?' she asked as they trotted through the park gates together.

* * *

Daisy and Leonie were hot and sticky, tired and thirsty when they flopped down on their backs under the horse chestnut tree after the hard fought match.

'Three-ee – two, three-ee – two!' Jared and Jimmy crowed as they went off arm in arm.

'We *let* you win!' Daisy shouted after them. 'But next time, don't count on us being so nice!'

The boys swaggered on regardless.

'Good game, so I don't mind losing,' Leonie sighed, staring up at the pattern of green leaves against the blue sky.

For a while Daisy let a contented silence develop. Then she broke it with the question that had been

bugging her since Friday.

'Leonie, what am I gonna do about Winona Jones?'

She'd thought carefully before raising the subject. Winona wasn't a topic you brought up lightly, since it could easily spoil the mood of the moment. But Daisy knew she could trust Leonie.

Reasons: 1) Leonie could sometimes run faster than Jimmy. 2) Leonie liked Legs. 3) Leonie and Daisy were on the same wavelength about schoolwork (ie. they both did as little as possible).

The list could have been longer, because the better Daisy got to know Leonie, the more she admired her.

For instance, Leonie didn't even have to try in order to succeed. Her long legs made her easily the best athlete in the school. In Art, she could take a piece of chicken wire and a bag of plaster and make a lifelike horse sculpture out of it in a single lesson. ('All by herself, with only a little advice from me!' Miss Ambler would boast to the school inspector.) This could have made Leonie a teacher's pet like Winona, but didn't.

Because the best thing about Leonie Flowers, and the quality which Daisy most envied in her, was that she had perfected the art of being naughty without *ever* getting into trouble.

So, when Daisy flopped under the tree and asked, 'Leonie, what am I gonna do about Winona Jones?', she expected sound advice.

The-girl-most-likely-to-succeed thought for a while. 'Well, you can't exactly stop her from trying to be your friend.'

Daisy acknowledged this. 'I know, I tried that. It doesn't work.'

Winona kept on popping up in her shiny black shoes, charming the pants off Daisy's parents.

Leonie thought some more, then came up with a brainwave.

'What you have to do is convert her. Make her change.'

Hmm, interesting. 'You mean, stop her from being Miss Ambler's pet and turn her into one of us?'

Leonie nodded. 'No more Saint Winona.'

Yeah! Daisy took the point. She admired Leonie's brilliant mind. 'Make her as bad as possible so she can join the gang? If we can get her into trouble and turn her into one of us, then end of problem!'

'Exactly!' Leonie rolled over on to her stomach to point out to Daisy that the subject of their conversation had just walked through the park gates with her pet poodle, Lulu.

Winona walked her dog at a distance. She carefully avoided yesterday's puddles and kept dainty Lulu on her nice red lead. The sun shone on her golden hair, fastened neatly into place with silver clasps.

'Hmm, could be difficult,' Daisy murmured. Winona was hardly a natural rebel. In fact, she was born to please.

'Yeah,' Leonie agreed, narrowing her dark brown eyes.

Winona the Good had never been told off in her entire life.

'Difficult but possible.' Daisy nodded. 'What we need now is a carefully worked out plan,' she said.

Three

'La-la, la-la-la!'

Winona Jones trilled a bright tune at Midge the school hamster.

Midge chomped hard on the scoop of grain and nuts which the pet-monitor had just tipped into her bowl. She puffed out her fat little cheeks and stored food for later – *stuff-stuff, munch-munch.*

It was Monday morning – and the start of the No-More-Saint-Winona project.

'Thank you for remembering to feed Midge, Winona dear,' Miss Ambler said, walking into the classroom with the register tucked under her arm.

'That's OK, Miss,' Winona replied in her sing-song voice. 'And please, Miss Ambler, may I clean out her cage at playtime?'

Leonie stole a glance at Daisy and made sick-noises.

'It's only because it's raining and she wants to stay in during morning break!' Daisy hissed.

But frumpy Miss Ambler in her flat shoes and frilly blouse was completely taken in by the Saint Winona routine. 'Of course you may, dear. Oh, and while I'm thinking about Midge, I've chosen you, Winona, to take her home and look after her during Spring Bank Holiday.'

'Miss, that's not fair!' Jade protested from her seat at the back of the room.

'Miss, we usually put our names in a box and the teacher draws one out,' Nathan patiently explained the process by which these things were done. He felt sorry for Miss Ambler because she was struggling towards the end of her first year in teaching.

'Winona did it last time!' Kyle Peterson pointed out.

'Not fair, not fair, not fair . . .' The low chorus rumbled around the room.

'La-la, la-la, la-la-la!' Winona hummed away with a smug smile.

'Children!' Miss Ambler put on her disapproving face and voice. With her head to one side and wearing a frown, she explained her bare-faced favouritism.

'Winona is my pet-monitor for the summer term, and she's been so good at her job that I've decided to reward her by letting her take Midge home again.'

'Not-fair-not-fair-not . . .' Rebellion rumbled on as the teacher plumped down at her desk and began to read names from the register.

For once, Daisy didn't join in the protests. Let Winona enjoy her moment of glory, she thought, since this is likely to be the last one she'll have for quite a while! Like, ever!

Sitting across the aisle in her seat by the window, Leonie caught Daisy's eye and nodded.

The Grand Plan, as agreed by Daisy and Leonie under the horse-chestnut tree in the park, was about to begin.

Step one: Miss Ambler would hand the completed register over to Saint Winona to take to the office as usual. (Besides being pet-monitor, Winona was also register monitor.)

Step two: Daisy would slip out at the same time, for some made-up reason. ('Please, Miss, I need the loo!'/ 'Miss Ambler, can I fetch Herbie from my coat pocket?'/ 'Miss, I forgot my packed lunch. May I go to the office and phone my mum?')

Step three: Daisy would waylay Winona and offer to take the register to Mrs Hannam for her. Even Winona would be happy to give up this boring job and make a speedy return to the classroom.

Step four: Daisy would deliberately 'forget' to deliver the register to the office. Mrs Hannam would panic. The whole school would be thrown into chaos by the hunt for Miss Ambler's class register. The register would later be 'found', dusty and bashed, behind a radiator in the assembly hall by Leonie.

Outcome: Winona would get the blame for failing to deliver the register as instructed. No one would believe her when she claimed she'd handed over the register to Daisy Morelli of all people.

Major disgrace. Mega loss of saintliness. Winona would be in the teachers' bad books for the first time in her entire life.

Steps One and Two went perfectly.

Winona and Daisy emerged from the classroom into the corridor at exactly the same time. ('Use the packed-lunch excuse.' Leonie had recommended. 'That one always works with Ambler!') Step Three also went the way it should.

'I'll take that!' Daisy seized the register from Winona and gave her a cheesy smile.

'How come?' Winona was suspicious.

''Cos I'm going to the office to make a phone call in any case. Why don't you nick off to the cloakroom for a couple of minutes?' (*Go comb your hair, polish your halo, why don't you*?)

Winona smiled back. 'OK, Daisy, thanks a lot. See you.' She scooted off down the corridor, innocently free of her duty.

It was Step Four where the problems occurred.

Daisy had the class register in her hot little hands. Now she had to stuff it down the back of the radiator in the hall, for Leonie to discover later.

So she snuck quietly past Mrs Hunt's classroom, hunched down so that no one could see her. Then she took a right turn into the assembly hall.

Tiptoe-tiptoe towards the chosen radiator, which was in the corner where the PE equipment was stored.

Daisy held her breath as she clambered over long benches and rolled-up rubber mats. If anyone saw her now, right this moment, she'd be in deep trouble . . .

'Sorry, no can do!' Mrs Hunt's classroom door opened and clicked shut again as Bernie King, the school caretaker, emerged into the corridor. As usual he was telling the teacher why he didn't have time to mend her window blind. 'I've got too much on; benches to set out for assembly, for a start!'

Oh no, not Bernie King! Daisy slithered off the mats, then ducked down behind the piano which was stashed away behind the PE benches. He would be with his black-and-white bulldog, Lennox, and, by the sound of the caretaker's jangling keys, the two of them were heading for the hall!

Pitter-pat, pitter-pat! The squat dog's claws rattled against the shiny red lino-tiles. Lennox the Bruiser, Lennox the wheezy, bad-breath heavyweight who waddled everywhere at his master's heels.

Clutching the register tight to her chest, Daisy squatted low behind the piano.

'Teachers!' Bernie King muttered as he entered the hall and made a bee-line for the benches. 'They must think I've got nothing to do all day!'

Huh-a, huh-a, huh! Lennox breathed hard and sniffed at the rubber mats.

'Down, boy!' Bernie commanded, lifting the first

bench, ready to set it out for assembly.

Sniff-sniff-sniff ! Lennox scaled the mat mountain.

Daisy could hear the dog's hot breath wheezing noisily at the side of the piano. Then his white face appeared, jaws drooling, little pink eyes homing in on her.

Wrr-ooo-ff! Half-growl, half-bark, Lennox gave a ferocious noise that made Daisy jump out of her skin.

Shaking from head to foot, she stood up.

'What the . . . ?' Bernie came over to investigate.

'Daisy Morelli, what the dickens are you doing there with that register?'

'I know, Mr King, I know!' Sorrowfully Miss Ambler shook her head and frowned at Daisy.

The caretaker and his dog had frog-marched the hideaway out of the hall, down the corridor and back to the classroom.

Bernie was in full flow. 'I might've guessed who it was skulking behind that piano!' he insisted. 'I don't know what it is about this particular girl, but somehow whenever there's trouble, I expect Daisy Morelli to be in the thick of it!'

Miss Ambler sighed and agreed.

Daisy stood in front of the whole class, kept at bay by a stern-looking Lennox. Her face burned with embarrassment.

When she snuck a glance around the room she could see Leonie with her gaze firmly fixed on the window, Jimmy looking worried for her, and Winona back at her desk looking pert and pink and squeaky-clean.

'If I were you I'd ask her what she was planning to do with that register!' King advised the rookie teacher. 'A register is an important official document. You can't just muck around and not take it to the office!'

'I know. I agree. Leave it with me,' Miss Ambler said, as firmly as she could.

So Bernie King went off grumbling, followed by a

panting Lennox. And the teacher turned her attention to Daisy. 'Daisy Morelli, don't even try to explain!'

'Please, Miss . . .'

'I said, don't!'

'No, Miss.' Daisy did her best to look upset, to work on the young teacher's soft side. Her dark hair fell forward to hide her face as she stared miserably at her shoes. Playing for sympathy was a long shot, but it might just work.

'It's one thing for Winona to agree to hand over the register when I'd sent her to the office with it . . .' Miss Ambler cast a sorrowful look in the direction of her star pupil. Winona's shiny smile faltered.

The teacher let Winona off the hook and turned back with a severe frown to the main culprit. 'But, Daisy, as Mr King quite rightly says, it's quite another for you to "muck around" with it in the assembly hall!'

'Yes, Miss.'

'And I don't even want to *know* what you planned to do with the register!' Miss Ambler's voice rose crossly as she glanced at her watch and saw that it was time for the class to file out to assembly.

'All I'm saying is that I agree with Mr King; if there's trouble in this school and we look around for the culprit, we never have to search far.

'Ask any one of the other teachers – Mrs Hunt, Mrs Waymann – who might be to blame and they all come up with the same answer. They don't even have to stop and think.

' "Who's the major troublemaker in Woodbridge Junior School?" Back comes the answer quick as a flash. "Daisy Morelli!" they tell me. "Yes, definitely Daisy!" '

Four

'OK, so the grand plan didn't work!' Leonie admitted.

She and Daisy managed to whisper a few words as they stood at the sink together, washing up paint materials after the art lesson.

'You can say that again,' Daisy moaned.

Not only had she been told off in front of the whole class – AGAIN! – but Winona had come out of the whole episode almost unharmed.

Worse still, Daisy's punishment was to stay in during every morning playtime this coming week!

('Why, Daisy; why?' Miss Ambler had sighed sadly over her naughty pupil. Then; 'No, don't tell me. I can't bear to hear your lame excuse!') 'So we have to think again!' Leonie insisted.

'Leonie Flowers, come away from that sink!' Miss Ambler ordered. 'Leave Daisy alone. It's time for you and the rest of the class to go out to play.'

Leonie managed a few final words without moving her lips.

Daisy noted yet another of Leonie's extraordinary talents.

'Like I say, we have to come up with another plan!' she hissed. (Actually, she said 'another Ian' since 'p' was impossible [*im-ossi-ul*] without moving her lips.)

'Leonie!' the teacher warned.

So Daisy's clever partner in crime dried her hands and went outside to snatch the world handstand record from her friend's grasp.

And Daisy herself took Herbie out of her drawer and sat with him in the corner of the classroom.

'We have to think of some other way of setting Winona up,' she said. 'So, any ideas?'

Herbie, hunkered on the window-sill, blinked back at her with his one beady eye.

Try letting Legs out of his jam-jar and claiming that it was Winona's fault. The hamster didn't speak out loud, but he was a whizz at telepathy.

Daisy's eyes lit up. 'Great idea!'

So she went straight across the empty classroom

to look in Nathan's drawer.

Unfortunately, Nathan and his spider were like Bernie King and Lennox; they went everywhere together. It stood to reason; the jar would be empty and Legs would be out enjoying the fresh air with the school's resident weirdo.

As she was retreating to Herbie's corner to consult with him again, Daisy caught sight of Midge trundling inside the exercise-wheel in her cage at the opposite end of the window-ledge.

'So where's Miss Win-oh-na now?' she said out loud. 'I thought she was supposed to be cleaning you out this playtime!'

Midge didn't reply. She just trundled.

'Any more ideas?' Daisy asked Herbie, picking him up and stroking him thoughtfully.

You could try planting a valuable item in Winona's drawer, then claiming she stole it.

Phew! That was big-time badness. Daisy didn't know if she was up to that.

'What *kind* of valuable item?' she asked, putting Herbie down on the ledge closer to Midge's cage. 'You mean, like someone's watch or dinner-money?'

Herbie scrunched up his squidgy face into an unreadable expression.

'No, you're right; too risky!' Daisy agreed swiftly. She whizzed Herbie smoothly along the sill, making him collide gently with the live hamster's cage.

Thud! Herbie came to a skidding halt.

Inside the cage, Midge got down from her wheel and came to check out what was going on. She poked her whiskery golden face against the wire-mesh and scrabbled at it with her front paws.

'Sorry, Midge!' Daisy apologised for upsetting the school hamster. 'It was only me messing around with Herbie.'

Picking up the beanie toy, she showed him to Midge. 'See, he's a hamster like you. Only he's not the real live kind, worse luck . . .'

Daisy held her hamster beside Midge, who squeaked a warning for the soft toy to keep off her patch.

'It's OK, he can't . . .' Daisy began.

From down the corridor, she heard the trip-trip-trip of dainty patent-leather shoes. So Winona hadn't forgotten about cleaning out Midge after all.

In the same moment, Daisy suddenly noticed something important.

'Y'know, Herb; you and Midge look pretty alike!' she whispered, staring from one to the other. 'You're both a kind of faded, fudgy-beige, not golden at all.'

But I have only one eye, Herbie reminded her.

'Yeah, yeah, forget that for a second. You're the same size and shape. In fact, you two could be twins!'

'Daisy, what are you doing?' Winona had opened

the classroom door and marched forward with a challenge. 'It's my job to clean Midge out, as you very well know!'

'I'm not – I wasn't!' Quickly Daisy fumbled Herbie behind her back and stepped to one side.

Winona sniffed and tossed her curls. 'Anyway, I decided to do it tomorrow instead of today.'

Daisy hardly took any notice. All she could think about was the fact that Herbie and Midge looked like twins!

Of course, it was only the germ of an idea and Daisy would have to work it out properly with Leonie, but – wow – this could be good!

In fact, it was better than good.

'If this works, Miss Ambler will never trust Winona Jones ever again!' Admiration for Daisy lit up Leonie's deep brown eyes.

' 'Course it'll work!' Daisy insisted.

She and Leonie had gathered in a huddle at the school gate first thing on Tuesday morning, along with Jimmy and Maya.

'So, run it by me.' Jimmy wanted to go over the plan yet again, ignoring the hordes of kids piling in through the gates.

Daisy went through events one more time.

'Our plan must be absolutely perfect,' the space station commander insisted to her tense crew. 'One small error will lead to total disaster!'

The three space travellers zipped up their silver suits and nodded nervously. They knew that their mission was important to the whole future of mankind.

Commander Morelli lowered her voice and spoke to each

one in turn. 'Scott, your job is to fire the booster rockets at the right nano-second. Greg, you keep a lookout for alien ships. And Zed, you may only be a robot, but you're programmed to have feelings just like us humans. So if you come under too much pressure, you must hand over control of the weapon system to me. Understood . . . ?'

'Got that!' Jimmy nodded as Daisy came to the end of the plan.

'OK, Maya?' Leonie checked. 'You think you can remember to open the french-window next to your desk during the science lesson without Miss Ambler noticing?'

Their small, dark-haired accomplice nodded eagerly. 'I can't wait till playtime!' she grinned, then ran off, her long plait swinging down her back.

It was the same for Daisy, Leonie and Jimmy; the build-up to break churned up their stomachs and made them tense with excitement. None of them had ever known the morning tick forward so slowly. Miss Ambler and her science lesson had never been so boring-snoring.

Brrrring!

The bell for playtime startled Daisy. The teacher broke off and the pupils slammed their books closed. Everyone, including Jimmy, Leonie and Maya, scraped back their chairs and made a headlong dash for the door.

'Not you, Daisy Morelli!' Miss Ambler shrieked above the noise. 'Your punishment was to miss every morning break this week, remember!'

'Yes, Miss Ambler,' Daisy said meekly.

So she stayed behind with Winona, who reminded Miss Ambler that her mission this playtime was to clean out Midge's cage.

'That's wonderful, dear,' the teacher murmured. 'It's so good of you not to mind giving up your break!'

So Winona waited until the classroom was empty except for Daisy, then she set to.

First she opened the hamster cage and lifted Midge out.

The fat little hamster squirmed in her cupped hands and wriggled as Winona carefully placed her inside the clear plastic ball which the school had bought specially.

The ball was about the size of a football and was made up of two halves which you unscrewed to open. The idea was to pop your pet hamster inside, screw the ball back together and put it somewhere safe while you cleaned the cage. Happy hamster would meanwhile trundle about contentedly inside the ball.

'There, Midge!' Winona cooed to the disgruntled school pet as she set her on the floor near to the door.

Midge was sulking about being inside the ball. She squatted and refused to move a muscle.

'So far, so good!' Daisy stayed in a far corner of the room, but kept a careful eye on what Winona was doing. Now it was time to quietly lift Herbie out of the corner of her drawer where she'd kept him well-hidden until he was needed.

Suddenly, as Winona got busy lifting the old wood shavings out of the cage, there was a loud rattle at the window.

'Hey, Winona!' Leonie knocked at the pane furthest away from the french window which led out into the playground. Her voice was faint through the glass. 'Come here a second!'

Winona scarcely looked up. 'Can't you see I'm busy?' she mouthed back.

'No, really; come over here!' Leonie acted as if she wanted to let Winona into a big secret. 'Kyle Peterson just told me he fancies you!'

'Ssshhh!' Winona dropped the shavings and ran to join Leonie, tugging the window open. 'Yuck, Kyle Stupid Peterson! Do you want the whole school to know?' she asked crossly.

'Kyle fancies you; he honestly does!' Leonie said gleefully.

Her big 'news' kept Winona occupied, as predicted.

Here was her chance! Daisy ran with Herbie to the

spot on the floor where Winona had placed the plastic cleaning-ball.

Rapidly unscrewing it, she took out Midge and replaced her with the beanie lookalike.

Now everything depended on Maya.

Holding a squirming Midge, Daisy raced to the french window.

Would it be unlatched? Would Maya be there in the playground, waiting as planned?

Yes! Quickly Daisy opened the door and secretly slid Midge out to Maya. Then she dashed back to the ball with Herbie inside, took hold of it and set it rolling at high speed.

'Sorry, Herbie!' she whispered, as the ball disappeared out of the door.

'Hey, Winona!' she yelled immediately afterwards in an innocent, frightened voice. 'Winona, look out!'

'What?' Turning away from her enthralling conversation with Leonie about revolting Kyle Peterson, Winona was just in time to see the cleaning-ball vanish through the door. 'Oh!'

She squealed and put both hands over her mouth.

'Midge set her ball rolling!' Daisy cried. 'She ran like mad inside. Her little legs were going like fury!'

'Why didn't you stop her?' Winona asked faintly, panic rooting her to the spot.

'Me?' Daisy flung her arms wide. 'So it was my job to look after Midge, was it? Funny; as pet-monitor, I thought that was down to you!'

Winona gasped and geared herself for action.

'Don't just stand there!' she yelled at Daisy. 'Which way did Midge go?'

'To the left, down the ramp leading to the staffroom!' Daisy declared.

It was hard to keep a straight face as she stepped to one side to let Winona out of the door. This whole thing was working perfectly.

'Poor Midge!' Winona cried, completely taken in by the trick.

Then, 'Oh, no; if she trundles the ball past the staffroom, Miss Ambler might see the whole thing and think I've been careless. Then I'll be in terrible, terrible trouble!'

Five

'All I did was to ask Mr King if he would mind mending the window blind in my classroom!' Mrs Hunt sighed over her cup of coffee during morning break. She was still cross over the caretaker's refusal to help the morning before.

'Bernie King is a law unto himself,' Miss Ambler sympathised.

She sat opposite the open staffroom door, gazing wearily into the corridor.

'As for his horrid, smelly dog . . .' Mrs Hunt moaned on.

'Good Lord!' Miss Ambler cut in. She put down her coffee and jumped to her feet.

'What is it?' Slower to react, the older teacher peered over her glasses in the direction of the open door.

'It was – no, it couldn't have been... there again, perhaps it could . . . !' Hesitating, stopping, then starting out into the corridor, Miss Ambler looked for the plastic hamster ball which, unless she'd been imagining things, had just trundled by.

Wumph! A frantic Winona Jones crashed into the puzzled teacher.

'Winona?' Miss Ambler took the full force of the blonde whirlwind chasing down the slope from the classroom. She dusted herself down then spoke severely. 'Correct me if I'm wrong, but wasn't that Midge I just saw rolling past the staffroom inside her cleaning-ball?'

Daisy could hardly keep the grin off her face.

She saw the crash between the teacher and her star pupil. She heard the tone of voice – 'Correct me if I'm wrong . . .' Waiting a split second before she put in an appearance, she sprinted down the slope. Her hair flew back from her face, her shirt flapped out of the waistband of her skirt. 'Poor Midge!' she gasped, laying it on thick. 'Her little head must be spinning inside that ball!'

'Daisy!' Miss Ambler commanded her to stop. 'What's going on? How did the hamster get out into the corridor?'

'Miss, I can't stop. I have to catch up with Midge!' Daisy protested.

By this time the ball containing Herbie had reached a short flight of steps down into the playground.

Bounce-bounce-bounce! It vanished down the steps, through the door and out of sight.

'Yes, of course.' The teacher took her point. 'Daisy, you carry on and bring the hamster back as fast as you can. Winona, you stay here. You and I need to have a little word!'

Brilliant! Superb! Excellent!

Daisy was busy congratulating herself and the whole gang.

Every detail had gone according to plan.

Space station commander to crew: All systems working perfectly. Repeat; all systems firing correctly. We're dead on course!

Relaxing now, she trotted down into the playground in time to see Jimmy in position, assuming a classic goalkeeper crouch.

He bent low, arms forward, palms wide, ready to catch the hamster cleaning-ball as it rolled across the tarmac towards him.

Trundle-trundle. The ball rattled and bumped over the hard surface. Inside, Herbie squidged and flopped against the clear sides. He looked for all the world like a dazed and dizzy, real live hamster.

'Oh, poor Midge!' kids gasped. The infants happened to be playing nearby and mistook the soft toy for the live animal.

One little boy from Reception Class cried loudly. 'Midge is dead!' he wept. 'I saw her, and she was all floppy!'

Ignoring all the kerfuffle, Daisy saw Jimmy crouch and wait until the last moment, then make a spectacular sideways dive.

'Good save!' Leonie cheered as Jimmy scooped up the ball.

'This way, Jimmy! Maya's waiting over by the bike shed!'

Perfect! Daisy jogged after Jimmy as he followed Leonie's directions.

Now all they had to do was complete the final stage of the plan.

Maya was waiting in the shed with Midge, as instructed. She had dashed with the hamster away from the french window, across the area of the playground marked out as a rounders pitch, and hidden away there until Daisy and Jimmy had carried out their parts.

Daisy had allowed one and a half minutes between swapping Herbie for Midge and this was the moment when all four plotters would meet up in the bike shed.

Another thirty seconds should see the second switch made.

Jimmy would hand the ball over to Daisy. Daisy would unscrew it and remove one crushed Herbie. Maya would pop Midge back into the ball. And while Leonie checked that the coast was clear, Daisy would screw the real hamster safe and sound back inside the cleaning-ball. Then the whole team would emerge and trot across the playground to loud cheers.

'Look, Daisy's gang saved Midge!'

'The hamster rolled all the way into the bike shed, wow!'

'I bet she's dizzy!'

'Winona Jones let her roll away!'

'Yeah, how dumb can you be?'

Daisy would carry Midge carefully on what would

feel like a lap of honour.

Then she would re-enter the school building solo and climb the steps to the staffroom. Flushed and proud, she would present Midge to Miss Ambler.

And Winona would be . . . DEAD!

'OK, Maya, where's Midge?' Leonie asked breathlessly.

Jimmy and Daisy were just entering the shadowy bike shed and quickly unscrewing the plastic ball.

'Quick!' Jimmy gasped, holding out the empty ball. If they took too long over this phase, people might get suspicious.

Daisy grabbed Herbie and stuffed him into her shirt pocket, where he bulged fatly.

'Maya?' Leonie demanded. She noticed Maya's look of dismay, then glanced down at her empty hands. 'Where's Midge?'

The question made Daisy's blood run cold. Her fingers fumbled to tuck Herbie completely out of sight.

Jimmy held out the two halves of the cleaning-ball, waiting in vain.

'Where's Midge?' Jimmy, Daisy and Leonie repeated as one.

Maya's bottom lip wobbled. Tears appeared at the rims of her enormous dark eyes and caught in her long, thick lashes. And the explanation came out in a trembly voice, bit by bit.

'She wriggled,' Maya began.

'Yeah?' Leonie challenged.

Maya nodded. 'Her claws were sharp.'

'So?' Jimmy pushed.

'Then she bit me!' Maya held up a finger to show them a bright red tooth-mark.

'You dropped her?' Daisy guessed. As she said the words, she felt her whole world collapse inwards like a deflated hot-air balloon.

Sssssss. Her plan was rocking wildly, sinking fast.

Maya choked, then nodded. 'Midge escaped!' she admitted. 'I'm sorry, Daisy. I really am!'

Six

'This definitely wasn't meant to happen!' Daisy felt like sagging to the ground and giving up. Her beautiful plan lay in ruins.

But Leonie managed to keep it together. 'Where *exactly* were you when Midge escaped?' she asked Maya.

'Over where Nathan is standing, by the netball post.' Unable to meet their eyes, Maya stood in the dark shed with eyes downcast, her long black plait drooped over one shoulder.

'So let's go look!' Leonie set off at a jog, cruising around the netball pitch, eyes peeled for a small, furry, golden hamster.

For a second Jimmy carried on staring at the empty plastic ball in his hands. Then he drew a deep breath and dumped it on Daisy. 'Over to you!' he said, speeding after Leonie in search of runaway Midge.

'What are you looking for?' Nathan asked in a loud, suspicious voice.

'Back off, Nathan!' Leonie said quietly.

'Yeah, watch out!' Jimmy circled Nathan and his hairy, pot-bellied pet.

Legs stretched, then meandered down the length of Nathan's arm.

Under cover of the bike shed, Maya whispered to Daisy, 'What are we gonna do?'

Daisy shook her head. 'Can hamsters survive in the wild?' she asked.

Pictures of Midge cowering under a rose bush in someone's garden while the neighbourhood cat stalked round and round caught hold of Daisy's lively imagination.

A scared hamster trembling. A black cat prowling closer and closer, claws out, body ready to spring. Shiny green eyes piercing. A round, furry face frozen with fear. A little heart racing – until suddenly it sounded one final thump and gave out . . .

It could happen, Daisy knew. And she felt the black hand of guilt clutch at her own heart and take away her breath. 'This is all my fault!' she whispered, her face white with dread, hands shaking.

'What will we tell Miss Ambler?' Maya asked.

The bell for the start of lessons had just gone and the playground was emptying fast. Meanwhile, Jimmy and Leonie continued to cruise around the area where Midge had disappeared.

Daisy considered Maya's frightened question, then gave her reply. Tucking the empty plastic ball under one arm and squaring her shoulders, she marched towards the school. 'I'll confess!' she announced nobly. 'I'm gonna tell Miss Ambler every single thing!'

'Not now, Daisy!' The teacher made it clear that she was too busy talking to Winona to listen.

With her friends around her, Daisy had held up the empty ball for all the class to see. She'd begun her full and frank confession. 'Midge escaped!'

A gasp had gone around the room. Everyone's gaze shot from the empty ball to the silent hamster cage in the corner.

Then Miss Ambler had cut her short. 'Can't you see that I'm trying to deal with Winona Jones? You'll have to wait!'

'B-b-but!' Daisy stammered.

'Yes, Daisy; I see that the hamster is missing. I'm not blind. I'm sure you, Maya, Leonie and Jimmy did your very best to stop it happening, and well done for trying. But now, just put the cleaning-ball on the window sill next to the cage and go and sit in your place.'

'W-w-we . . . I mean, I . . . I didn't mean for Midge to escape!' Daisy made what she thought was a clean breast of it. She waited for the teacher's angry response.

'No, Daisy, dear. None of us wanted to lose our lovely little hamster. And I'm sure we all know who to blame!' Miss Ambler shooed the gang back to their seats, then returned to her attack.

'I must say, Winona, that I'm very, *very* disappointed in you!'

Standing at the front of the room, Winona hung her

head awkwardly but said nothing.

'I trusted you – the whole class trusted you – to take good care of Midge. And what happened? A moment of pure carelessness when you turned your back and let her set the ball in motion, that's what happened!'

As Miss Ambler lectured hard, Daisy studied Winona's half-hidden face. She could see that she was red and trying not to cry. Even her blonde curls seemed to have drooped and lost their shine.

'One small careless action,' the teacher continued. 'But look at the result. Poor Midge is lost and we may never find her alive again!'

A shiver ran round the class. Someone on the front row sniffled quietly.

'I'm sorry, Miss Ambler,' Winona said in a tiny voice.

The teacher glared and delayed for maximum effect. Finally she delivered her verdict. 'On this occasion, Winona, I think I speak for everyone here when I tell you that sorry is not enough!'

'Well, our plan worked, didn't it?'

It was home-time and Leonie stood at the school gates pointing out the obvious to Jimmy, Maya and Daisy.

'Oh sure, it worked!' Jimmy said scornfully. 'Midge has only vanished, that's all!'

'I mean, we got Winona into Ambler's bad books, like

we wanted,' Leonie insisted. 'She even had to go and see Waymann, remember!'

But Leonie's reminder fell strangely flat. Daisy recalled Winona's white, dull face as she'd trailed off to see the head teacher for one of her famous 'little words'. It was as if a bomb had dropped into Winona's world and left her shell-shocked.

Then, when she'd come back, Daisy had noticed with a rush of shame that Winona's eyes and nose were red from crying and she'd spent the rest of the afternoon with her head buried in the book she'd chosen from the library.

And now, after school, poor Winona was coming out of the building by herself, with no spring in her step, trying her best to avoid other kids from the class.

Poor Winona! Daisy pulled herself up short. *What am I saying; poor Winona?* Hadn't Miss Perfect made Daisy's own life a misery until now, with her unasked-for advice and superglue habit of sticking around where she wasn't wanted?

And now that the Midge incident had successfully pulled Winona down by several pegs, surely she would be less big-headed and goody-goody in future?

After all, that's the whole point! Daisy told herself firmly.

Poor Winona nothing! The hamster plot would all work out fine in the end. If only . . .

'If only we could find Midge!' Jimmy sighed, as if reading Daisy's thoughts.

Super-practical Leonie stepped in with a suggestion. 'Let's form a search party!'

'When?' Maya asked.

'Now!' Leonie shot back.

'Good idea,' Jimmy agreed.

So Leonie stood on the wall and asked for volunteers to stay behind and help find the missing hamster.

'Me; I will!' Jade offered, after checking with her big sister to see if it would be OK.

'Count me in,' Kyle piped up, giving Winona a

sympathetic smile as she trailed by. 'How about you?' he asked her.

Winona shook her head. 'No, I have to go straight home or my mum will be worried,' she sighed.

Daisy felt another pang of guilt as she watched Winona leave, head bowed, patent-leather shoes scuffing slowly along the pavement. *Tomorrow! she promised silently. Tomorrow I'll confess everything to Miss Ambler!*

And by that time, with a bit of luck, they would have found Midge.

'I'd like to volunteer!' Nathan told Leonie. Which meant that Daisy, Jimmy, Leonie, Maya, Jade, Kyle and Nathan made up the search party.

'Where do we start?' Kyle asked, gazing around the vast playground. 'Where would Midge hide?'

'She could have scooted back into school,' Jade suggested.

'Hamsters like warm places.'

So Leonie told Jade and Kyle to search the entrance and the steps leading up to the staffroom. 'If Bernie King tries to chuck you out, tell him we're the official Midge search party and we've got permission to be in school.'

Kyle looked doubtful. 'Have we?'

'No. But Bernie won't know that, will he?' Leonie turned quickly to Maya and Jimmy. 'I think you two should check the bike shed.'

They nodded and sprinted across the yard.

'Daisy, you and I need to search outside the gates, along Woodbridge Road.' Leonie was in total charge now, thinking things through and positive that all would soon be well.

So Daisy fell in with her orders, until Nathan stepped across their path and blocked their way.

'What about me?' he demanded, stony-faced. 'You didn't give me anything to do.'

'Oh, Nathan, right!' Leonie hesitated. What good would a geek like Nathan be, balancing along wall tops and peering into gardens? 'I know, you can go and join Kyle and Jade inside the building.'

Nathan stood his ground. His faded fair hair flopped over his forehead and stuck out at all angles from the top of his head, like he had a permanent electric shock. 'I'd rather be outside with you and Daisy,' he insisted.

'OK, but don't hold us back,' Leonie agreed, knowing there was no time to argue.

So the three of them set off down the street, stopping to ask the crossing-lady, then the man who owned the newsagents next door to the school. 'Did you see a runaway hamster earlier today by any chance?'

'No, sorry,' came the answer. Or, 'What does it look like . . . small, fat, fudge-coloured? . . . No, sorry!'

Five minutes passed and they'd had no luck at all.

And it turned out that Nathan wasn't much help either. 'Waste of time asking these questions,' he mumbled, taking Legs out of his jam-jar and making tweeting noises at him with puckered lips. 'What we need to do is look for clues.'

'What *kind* of clues?' Daisy wanted to know. She and Nathan were waiting for Leonie, who had disappeared into yet another shop.

'Pawprints, droppings, that scientific kind of thing,' Nathan replied.

Daisy's jaw dropped. 'You're not serious!' How small were a hamster's pawprints? What chance did they have of spotting any on a stone pavement?

Nathan frowned. 'Deadly serious,' he insisted, thoughtfully stroking Legs. Then he pointed at the lumpy, squidgy, fudge-coloured object half poking out of Daisy's shirt pocket. 'Anyway, Daisy Morelli, why are you carrying Herbie around everywhere all squidged up like that?'

Seven

'Umm . . . er . . . um.' For once Daisy was lost for words.

Nathan narrowed his eyes behind the smudged lenses of his taped-up glasses. 'For a second you had me fooled into thinking that Herbie was Midge.'

'Ha! No way!' She felt a hot flush cover her whole body. Was Nathan's casual comment a fluke, or did he know something?

The school boffin continued his weirdly accurate train of thought. 'I mean, Herbie and Midge do look alike. It would be easy to mistake one for the other . . .'

'Like, yeah!' Daisy did her best to scoff. 'Only *you* would think that, Nathan!'

Luckily Leonie came out of the shop just at that moment. She held up a bar of nut chocolate. 'I bought this to tempt Midge out of hiding,' she explained. 'I think it's time we went back to school and re-grouped.'

So the three of them re-traced their steps along Woodbridge Road, still searching under hedges and in litter bins as they went along, asking anyone who would listen if they had seen a runaway hamster.

No – No – No. The answer was always the same.

'Well, that was a complete waste of time,' Nathan said, as they ran back through the school gates.

'No need to sound so smug,' Leonie grumbled.

Yeah, Nathan, Daisy thought. How come you're not the least bit worried about what happened to Midge? She didn't say anything, but her questions about the strange boy's attitude were mounting. For instance, why had he offered to join the search party if he couldn't care less about the hamster? And why was he grinning secretly to himself as Jimmy and Maya came trotting across the playground to inform Leonie that there was no sign of Midge in the bike shed?

'Out!' a voice boomed from inside the school.

Jimmy, Maya, Daisy, Leonie and Nathan swung round just in time to see Kyle and Jade charging down the stone steps. They tripped and tumbled over themselves in their haste.

'The King has spoken!' Leonie recognised the hand

of the grumpy caretaker behind the rapid exit.

And sure enough, the squat figures of Bernie King and Lennox soon appeared in the doorway. Man and dog loomed over the two quivering kids.

'Who gave you permission to come snooping round school after the bell's gone?' Bernie demanded, folding his thick arms and filling up the entire door frame.

Wrrroooffff! Lennox lent his support. His jowls slavered, his mean pink, piggy eyes fixed on a quaking Jade.

Then the caretaker's gaze lifted and he took in the rest of the search party in the playground. 'Let's see, who else is involved in this latest little scam . . . Ah yes, Jimmy Black, Leonie Flowers, Daisy Morelli . . . the usual suspects!'

Daisy spoke up for the gang. 'We're only trying to find...'

'Save the excuses!' King boomed. 'I'll be making a note of all your names and passing them on to Mrs Waymann first thing in the morning.'

Wrroof-wrrooff! Lennox agreed.

Then the caretaker spotted Nathan. 'That doesn't include you, sonny. I know you can't possibly be mixed up with this hopeless lot.'

Nathan stared back, saying nothing but obviously thinking plenty.

What's going on inside that weird head? Daisy wondered.

'So go on, clear off!' King ordered.

Lennox dribbled and took a couple of steps forward.

There was no arguing with an overweight bulldog, so they retreated to the pavement outside the main gates.

'What now?' Jimmy asked impatiently. It was high time for him to be kicking a ball about in the park.

Leonie knitted her smooth brown eyebrows. 'Looks like we're stuck,' she muttered, shoving Midge's chocolate treat into her pocket. 'We'll just have to call off the search until tomorrow morning.'

Reluctantly, the others agreed, though Jade worried about Midge being out alone overnight and Kyle pointed out that every hour that went by was vital. Daisy sighed and admitted that there was nothing more they could do.

'Bye!' Jimmy said, the first to split. 'See ya!'

'Bye!' Jade and Kyle went off a different way.

'Sorry, Daisy,' Maya murmured for the hundredth time.

' 'Snot your fault. See you tomorrow.' She watched Maya and Leonie team up and head for home.

Which left her and Nathan standing by the school gate.

Daisy was about to beat a hasty retreat from the school nerd when Nathan said something really odd, even for him.

'So Daisy, how much does it mean to you to get

Midge back in one piece?' His faded grey eyes stared at her, his voice was low and fast.

'Huh?' It took her a few seconds to realise that he was offering to do some kind of deal. 'Nathan, what's going on?'

'It's a simple question,' he insisted, squaring his shoulders and swaggering. 'I take it that the hamster means a lot to you?'

'Nathan, why are you coming across with this stupid gangster stuff?' Daisy's voice rose in protest. 'You can cut the American accent for a start!'

He shrugged and turned away. 'So, be like that.'

Daisy stepped across his path. 'No, sorry, Nathan. I

didn't mean . . .' She gave in and decided to play it his way. 'OK, what's the deal?'

A faint smile played over Nathan's freckled face. 'The deal is, I get to join the gang.'

'*You*?' Daisy stepped back. The school geek, the maths and science genius, the kid who kept pet spiders, wanted to become one of them? 'Nathan, don't try to be funny!'

'I'm not laughing. I mean it, so you can close your mouth and stop gawping, Daisy Morelli.' Nathan snapped out his final demand. If Daisy didn't play it his way, he would simply turn his back and walk away. 'Listen, if you want to know what happened to the precious hamster, you have to let me join the gang!'

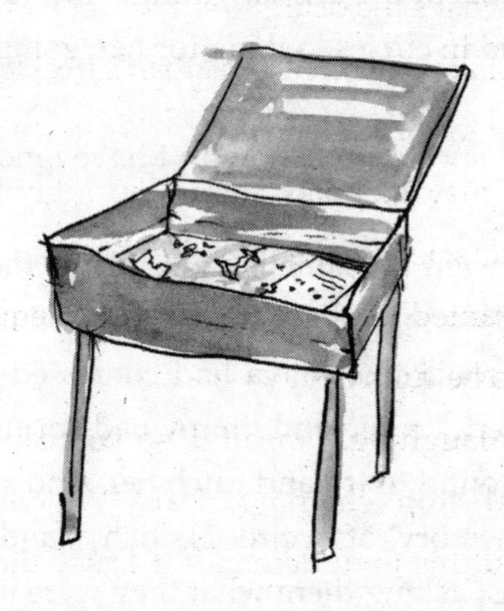

Eight

'That's blackmail!' Daisy protested. Suddenly she was seeing Nathan Moss in a new and chilly light.

'Yep,' he agreed.

'What are you saying? You know what happened to Midge?'

'Yep.'

'You've known all along?' Daisy's voice rose to a squeak.

'Yep.'

'What's more; you know where she is right this very minute?'

'You've got it,' Nathan confirmed. He let Legs out

of his jar and up on to his shoulder.

'And you didn't say anything? You just let us all run around in circles looking for her, going crazy with worry?'

'Leonie and Jimmy shouldn't have ignored me,' he said coolly.

'If you want to blame anyone, blame them.'

Daisy thought back to the moment when the grand plan had collapsed. Maya had confessed that Midge had escaped, Leonie and Jimmy had sprinted out into the playground to try and catch her. And yes! She had a clear memory of weird Nathan standing by the netball post asking them what they were looking for.

'Back off, Nathan!' Leonie had yelled.

'Yeah, watch out!' Jimmy had cruised around him in a wide circle, looking anxiously for the missing pet.

'If they'd told me what they were doing, I could've helped,' he said calmly yet mysteriously.

Daisy let out a loud sigh. 'OK, give it to me straight, Nathan,' she said wearily.

'I saw it all,' he explained. 'I watched Maya take Midge from you and run to the bike shed. I watched Jimmy catch the cleaning-ball with Herbie inside. I heard Maya yell "ouch!" and drop the hamster. Midge made a bee-line for me. All I had to do was pick her up and pop her into Legs' jam-jar. Simple as that.'

'OK, you win. You can join the gang!' Daisy

admitted defeat.

She was still reeling from the shock of Nathan's news when who should show up at the end of Woodbridge Road but Winona Jones.

All the more reason to keep things moving.

'So tell me where Midge is now!' Daisy begged.

'She's in a cardboard box inside my classroom drawer,' Nathan told her, very laid-back. He too had spotted Winona.

'C'mon, let's go and get her out of there!' Daisy grabbed Nathan by the shirt sleeve and tried to drag him towards the school.

But Nathan acted like they had all the time in the world.

'Don't you owe a certain person an apology first?'

'Not now. Later!' Daisy panicked at the idea of having to eyeball Winona and tell her everything. Tomorrow, face to face with Miss Ambler would be soon enough for the Big Confession.

'Yoo-hoo, you two!' Winona waved at them. There was a bounce back in her stride and a gutsy look on her face. 'It's OK, I've been home and checked in with my mum. She gave me permission to come and join in the search for Midge!'

Daisy groaned as Winona drew near.

'Don't worry, we'll find her in the end,' Winona promised kindly, misunderstanding the reason behind Daisy's moan of despair. 'It stands to reason, a hamster can't just vanish into thin air!'

'Oh, Daisy!' The shock and hurt on Winona's face when she heard the full confession was difficult to bear.

'I'm sorry!' Daisy whispered.

Nightmare! How had it all gone so wrong? Was this her just reward for being mean to Winona? Did the universe really operate in that organised a way?

Nathan stood by with an air of quiet satisfaction, while Legs took a stroll across his chest. 'Maybe Winona would like to join the gang as well,' he suggested.

Daisy gulped, then turned to Winona. 'Would you?'

Winona's blue eyes shone. A dream come true. 'Could I *really*?'

Daisy nodded. 'On one condition.'

'Which is?'

'You have to learn to be bad. I mean, really, really bad!' As Leonie had said, 'No more Saint Winona!'

'You mean, like you?' Winona considered the challenge. 'I'd have to do horrible stuff with superglue and secret notes; that kind of thing?'

Daisy nodded. 'What d'you think? Can you do it?'

Winona took a deep breath then came up with her answer. 'I could try!'

'Mr King, is it OK if Nathan, Daisy and I slip back into the classroom, please?' Winona started as she meant to continue from now on by wheedling her way past the school janitor.

'What for?' came the gruff, grunting reply. Fat Lennox sat wheezily to heel outside his master's damp basement office.

'Erm, we just forgot something important,' Winona told him.

'It's way past home time,' Bernie pointed out, his eyes narrowing suspiciously. 'I've already told Daisy Morelli to make herself scarce.'

Winona ignored the Daisy remark. 'We thought we'd better ask your permission, Mr King,' she said sweetly. 'Nathan needs to collect his trumpet for Music Centre. I have to pick up a book for my English homework and Daisy – er, Daisy needs something from her drawer.'

King sniffed grudgingly. 'You and Nathan can go ahead, no problem. But I wouldn't trust Daisy Morelli as far as I could throw her.'

So Winona and Nathan had to leave Daisy sulking by the main door while they went into the deserted school to rescue Midge from Nathan's drawer.

'It's not fair!' Daisy muttered to herself, all the events of the day had been building to this point, and now, just because of Bernie-the-Bully King's suspicious mind, she was forced to miss it.

But wait! She remembered the french window leading into the classroom from the playground. If she scooted around and knocked on the window, Nathan and Winona would be able to let her in. She would be in on the finale after all.

So she sprinted around corners, ducking low past Bernie King's office, ignoring Lennox's throaty growl. And she arrived at the french window just in time to see Winona and Nathan enter the classroom by the more usual route.

'Psst!' She hissed, then tapped lightly at the window.

Winona spotted her and immediately opened the glass door.

'Good thinking, Daisy!'

'So, c'mon, Nathan, open your drawer!' Daisy was impatient to see Midge with her own eyes.

But he took his time, whisking his hands in front of the drawer like a magician about to draw a rabbit out of a top-hat. 'Da-dah!' he cried, then slid the drawer out of its slot.

Empty!

Well, actually, full of chewed paper and wax crayons and a wrecked cardboard box with hamster teeth-marks all over it.

But no actual hamster.

'Oh!' Winona peered inside the drawer in dismay.

Nathan leaned forward and pulled out one semi-digested maths project. He studied it in horror. 'Ambler will kill me!' he breathed.

'OK, Einstein, what now?' Daisy stood with her hands on her hips, demanding the next genius-move.

All three stood for a while in silent dismay.

Then Daisy heard a squeaking, creaking, trundling noise from the window sill.

Squeak-squeak, creak-creak, trundle-trundle.

The sound of a hamster using an exercise wheel.

'Midge!' they cried, and dashed to the hamster's cage.

The door was open and a cloud of dusty wood shavings was being raised as the exercise wheel spun round.

Squeak-squeak-squeak! The wheel turned. And a small, furry face peered out at the astonished trio.

'Midge, you're safe! You found your own way back!' Winona breathed.

Creak-creak! The hamster trundled on.

'Nice one, Midge!' Nathan grunted. 'But what about my maths project?'

Daisy just grinned and thought of what she would tell the gang.

Trundle-trundle.

Space station commander to crew. Midge returned to base.

Mission accomplished. I repeat, mission accomplished!

You must be joking, Jimmy!

Jenny Oldfield

Illustrated by
Lauren Child

One

'A tattoo?' Daisy echoed. She stared hard at her friend, Jimmy Black. 'A real tattoo?'

'Yeah, why not?' Jimmy shrugged. 'Tattoos are cool.'

'B-b-but . . . !'

'Way to go, Leonie!' Jade, Jared, Kyle and Maya cheered loudly as Leonie picked up her last potato, popped it in her sack, then sprinted for the finish-tape.

'B-b-but . . . !' Daisy was still spluttering when Leonie burst through the tape ten yards ahead of her nearest rival. 'What's the tattoo of? Where is it? How big?'

Jimmy tossed his head so that his floppy brown hair flipped back from his forehead. He stood up from the grass and set off strolling towards the start of the obstacle race. Weaving in and out of the crowd of kids and parents all gathered on the playing-field for the school sports day, he paused to wait for Daisy.

'I didn't say I'd *got* a tattoo,' he explained. 'What I said was, I *wanted* one!'

'A tattoo?' Winona Jones elbowed her way into their conversation. She joined Jimmy and Daisy dressed in the whitest pair of shorts, the best pressed T-shirt and the most expensive trainers money could buy. 'Oh, puh-lease!' she smirked. 'What a joke!'

'Butt out, Win-oh-na!' Daisy snapped. 'So, Jimmy, why do you want this tattoo?'

'All those children who have been entered for the obstacle race, please take their positions at the start!' Mrs Hunt announced wearily over the loudspeaker. It had been a long, tiring afternoon for the elderly teacher.

At the far end of the course, young Miss Ambler stood ready to record the winners in her diary. Her long, dark blue cotton skirt billowed in the wind, revealing a pair of cheesy-white legs.

'I want a tattoo because Robbie Exley just got one done on his right shoulder blade.' Jimmy came clean with the reason.

'Yeah, but . . .' Daisy still couldn't put her thoughts into words. 'A *real* tattoo!'

'Take your positions,' Mrs Hunt repeated in a tinny voice.

Jimmy lined up next to Daisy, with Winona on his far side. 'I want a lion roaring, with its mouth wide open,' he whispered earnestly. 'Just like Robbie.'

Super-Rob, the Steelers' ace goal-scorer. Robbie Exley, Jimmy's all-time soccer hero. If Robbie had a tattoo, then that explained everything.

In lane three Winona snorted and shook her blonde head.

'Next thing, you'll be having your hair cropped to a stubble and wearing an ear-stud!' Daisy warned. She didn't think that a lion tattoo would suit shy Jimmy. Nor did she think it would fit on his skinny shoulder-blade. But she decided not to tell him up front in case it hurt his feelings.

'Would Nathan Moss please hurry and line up at the start of the obstacle race!' Mrs Hunt whined over the megaphone. 'Nathan? . . . Has anyone seen Nathan Moss?'

Meanwhile Bernie King, the school caretaker, stood with a bright green flag raised high over his head, ready to sweep it down to the ground for the start of the final race of the day. Fat Lennox, his asthmatic white bulldog, sat wheezily at his side.

'What's wrong with me having a tattoo?' Jimmy demanded, his face flushing red and growing stubborn.

'Nothing!' Daisy assured him.

Winona snorted and swallowed a giggle.

'. . . Ah, there you are, Nathan!' Mrs Hunt sighed, then signalled to Bernie King that they were ready at last.

Nathan had appeared out of the crowd in a pair of too-big, borrowed trainers. His wild, straw-coloured hair stuck up as usual, but he was minus his taped-up glasses and minus Legs, his pet spider.

'Jimmy Black says he wants a tattoo!' Winona sniggered to Nathan.

Nathan blinked back. 'Weird!' he muttered.

'What's weird about it?' Daisy stuck up for her best friend. 'If Jimmy wants a tattoo like Robbie Exley's, what's to stop him?'

'Ready!' Bernie roared, flag poised.

'The law,' Nathan pointed out coolly. 'That's what's to stop him. Jimmy's only nine. He can't have a tattoo without his parents' permission!'

The news shocked and dismayed poor Jimmy. 'Is that true?'

'Yeah, course. Didn't you know that?' Winona sniggered.

'On your marks, get set . . . !' The King of Woodbridge Junior roared the commands. Lennox coughed and wheezed all over Nathan.

'Is it?' Jimmy whispered to Daisy.

Shoving her untidy mass of long, dark hair behind

her ears, Daisy leaned forward, ready to dash. Know-all Nathan was always right. 'I guess so,' she admitted.

'. . . Go!' Bernie barked.

And twelve reluctant kids sprinted for the first obstacle while a crowd of so-called grown-ups screamed blue murder and egged them on.

'Nathan Moss!' Painstakingly Miss Ambler noted down the winner, while Daisy, Jimmy and the rest still struggled through a bright blue plastic tunnel towards the finish-tape.

Would Daisy's lungs take the strain? Would she be able to hold her breath in this underwater cave, grasp the gleaming pearl from the pink depths of the oyster shell, fight her way through the jungle of seaweed, past the tentacles of the humungous octopus and break the surface without gasping for non-existent air? Glug-glug-glug. The bubbles rose, her eyes almost popped out of her head as she fought her way through.

'Second, Winona Jones!' Miss Ambler recorded the runner-up.

Back in the blue tunnel, Daisy elbowed her way past Kyle Peterson.

'Ouch!' Kyle yelped and rolled to one side. 'Help! Daisy Morelli just sat on me. Now I'm stuck!'

Glug-glug! Almost there. The pearl was priceless. It would make Daisy wealthy beyond her wildest dreams . . .

'Third, Jade Harrison!' Her duty finished, Miss Ambler put her diary on a nearby plastic chair. She ran to rescue Kyle, who, to judge by the muffled yelps and cries, seemed to have collapsed in the tunnel.

Whoosh! Pearl in hand, Daisy burst from the exit and took a great gulp of air.

Miss Ambler dropped on to her hands and knees to peer inside the blue tube. 'Kyle,' she called. 'Where are you? Are you all right?'

'Please Miss, I'm stuck!' came the muffled reply.

Sprinting for the finish-line, Daisy came up alongside Jimmy.

'Who won?' she gasped. Maybe her ears had been deceiving her when Miss Ambler had called Nathan's name. Geeky Nathan couldn't run or climb things to save his life. Could he?

'Nathan Moss,' Jimmy grunted, his arms going like pistons as he pounded over the last ten metres.

'C'mon, Daisy *mia*! R-r-run, run, run, my bambina!'

Daisy cringed as she heard her dad's lilting voice soar above the rest.

Wow, was this embarrassing. Her dad, Gianni, yelling and drawing attention to her as she came a lame fifth after Jimmy. 'Go home and make pizza!' she muttered to herself. 'Chop onions, make tomato sauce, grate cheese – anything!'

But her dad grabbed her as she crossed the line and gave her one of his big bear-hugs. 'Never mind the winning,' he grinned. 'It's the taking part that counts!'

With a *real* priceless pearl Daisy would buy her mum and dad the biggest pizza restaurant in the world, she decided, as she watched Nathan go up to Mrs Hunt to record his winning time.

The Pizza Palazzo would be a *real* palace, not just a little shop on Duke Street. It would be made of pink and white marble, the taps on the sinks would be solid gold . . .

All around, parents were claiming their kids and carting them off to their cars.

'Well done, dear.'

'. . . Never mind, don't cry.'

'What happened, Kyle? Did someone deliberately injure you . . . ?'

Quickly Daisy dodged out of her dad's embrace. She slipped away to help Jimmy stack plastic chairs.

'Erm, if anyone would care to stay behind and help us to clear up, we'd be most grateful!' Mrs Hunt whinged through the megaphone.

'Hey!' Jimmy said suddenly. He seized a black

book from one of the chairs and opened it. 'This is Rambler-Ambler's diary!'

'Let me see!' Daisy pounced, snatched it from him and read the gold lettering on the cover. Sure enough: WEEK-TO-VIEW DIARY. Inside, on the very first page, above the list of times for sunrise and sunset, she made out the name, Louise Ambler.

'Louise!' Daisy crowed.

'Daisy *mia,* come quick. We have to go home and open the Palazzo. People want pizza!' her dad called from the gate.

'Coming!' she called back. 'Jimmy, did you see this? Boring-Snoring's first name is Louise!'

'Jimmy, Daisy, what are you two up to?' Mrs Hunt had crept up on them unexpectedly, megaphone in hand.

'Nothing!' Jimmy jumped a mile.

Daisy whipped the diary behind her back and assumed an innocent air.

'Hmm.' The teacher looked at them suspiciously. 'Run along home,' she said shortly. 'No, Jimmy, don't argue. And Daisy, have you gone deaf? Didn't you hear your father calling you?'

'B-b-but!' It was Daisy's day for stammering and stuttering. How could she put back Miss Ambler's diary without facing some serious questioning?

(". . . Daisy Morelli, why were you prying into Miss Ambler's private diary? . . . Daisy, tut-tut, what are you doing poking your nose into Miss Ambler's personal affairs? . . . Mr and Mrs Morelli, I'm afraid your daughter has got herself into serious trouble yet again!")

'Go along!' Mrs Hunt threatened, sounding tired and frazzled.

In the distance, Miss Ambler was busy collapsing the long blue tube and folding it up.

'C'mon, Daisy!' Jimmy grunted through gritted teeth.

'B-b-but . . . !' Oh, this was hopeless.

So Daisy shoved the stupid diary into the back waistband of her shorts, covered it with her T-shirt, then turned and ran for the gate.

Two

The black book was a doorway into Miss Ambler's life beyond school. An illegal but fascinating glance behind the scenes. And it had fallen into Daisy's ownership almost by accident.

Holding the diary between her hands in the privacy of her own bedroom, Daisy's fingers trembled.

'SCHOOL SHOCKER!' Daisy could see the headlines now, after she had gone public and blown the gaff on her teacher's secret life. 'TEACHER TRAINS TIGERS IN SPARE TIME!' Or, 'JUNIOR SCHOOL TEACHER STARS IN BRITISH SCI-FI EPIC! Louise Ambler, alias Princess Nola in Asteroid Army, takes on the entire forces of far-flung planet Likos single-handedly in a forthcoming blockbuster movie.

'She overcomes three thousand Likosians with her superior IQ and the skilled use of her laser-sword, forces entry into the inner sanctum of the Los, the handsome Likosian ruler, and finally persuades him through her beauty and her silver-tongued charm to submit to the authority of Queen Tara and her Galactic Guard . . .' This was *before* Miss Rambler Ambler had switched jobs and become the most boring teacher in the universe, of course.

Miss Boring Snoring. Bad career move, as things turned out, when, if she'd stuck with acting, Louise could have had all Hollywood at her feet.

'Daisy, have you finished your homework?' her mum called up the stairs.

'Yep,' she lied. In fact, she planned to borrow Leonie's maths book on the way to school tomorrow morning and crib the answers from her stunningly clever and generous friend.

'Supper will be ready in five minutes . . . Daisy, did you hear me?'

'Uh? What? . . . OK!' With shaking hands she opened up the diary and turned to the middle pages.

'July 2, Monday – Send off SAT test results. Phone mother. Wash hair in evening.' Major let-down. Daisy flicked to the bottom of the next page and tried again.

'July 6, Friday.' This would be better. Friday would be Louise's day to go clubbing, meet up with her girlfriends, get drunk and let down her mousy hair.

'Buy new M & S blouse for school (cream, size 12, to go with dark blue skirt).
Dentist's appointment, 4.45pm.' And that was it for that week. Major, major disappointment.

'. . . Daisy, supper!' Angie Morelli called.

'Coming! Just let me finish my last maths sum!'

'I thought you said you'd done your homework?'

'What? Oh yeah. Sorry. I have. Coming!'

Trying but failing to slip the small black book into her trouser pocket, Daisy hid it instead under her pillow next to beanie babe Herbie and went downstairs without it.

'And this is my own favourite dish: Pizza Gianni!' Daisy's dad charmed the money out of his customers' pockets as Daisy went through the restaurant into the kitchen to find her mum.

'Pizza *al funghi* with crushed garlic – mmm! – fresh herbs and a mountain of *formaggio* all melted to a delicious crispy topping on a deep-pan base!'

'It sounds wonderful!' the young couple sitting at the window table murmured, gazing into each other's eyes over a single red rose.

'Beans-on-cheese-on-toast!' Angie announced the menu for Daisy's own supper. 'On the worktop.' She didn't turn round because she was in the middle of playing aeroplanes with baby Mia's apple-and-custard pudding.

'*Neeee-aaahhh*!' Angie held the loaded spoon poised eighteen inches above Mia's head. Then she swept her hand down like a jet-fighter, making plane noises.

Mia cooed, gurgled, then opened her mouth just as the spoon dipped by. *Gulp*. The pudding was gone.

'Good girl!' Daisy's mum murmured. 'More?'

Meanwhile, Daisy grabbed her plate. Beans-on-cheese-on-toast was her own favourite dish. No crushed garlic, no fresh herbs to spoil things . . .

'Don't gobble,' her mum said without looking.

A fork full of beans from the tin plate, swilled down with strong black coffee, then saddle up your horse and hit the trail.

This was the cowboy's life . . .

'Close your mouth while you're eating,' Angie ordered. Then '*Nee-aagghhh* – *gulp*!' Another plane found its target.

'How come Mia can eat with her mouth wide open?' Daisy protested.

'Don't talk with your mouth full!'

Daisy gave up and scoffed her soggy toast,

jumping up from the table just as her mum lifted Mia out of her baby-seat and prepared to take her upstairs to the flat. Angie sat Mia on her hip and followed Daisy upstairs, wading into her room after her through heaps of magazines and comics which lay strewn across the floor.

'Any stray laundry?' her mum asked, swooping on the grass-stained shorts at the foot of Daisy's bed.

Mia enjoyed the roller-coaster ride. 'Goo-goo-ca-choo!'

'What about your bedclothes?' Angie demanded. She pounced on the nearest pillow.

There lay Miss Ambler's little black book beside a crushed Herbie hamster. *Disaster!*

'What's that?'

'Nothing!'

Daisy leapt on to the bed from the far side of the room. She grabbed the diary before her mum could pick it up, knocking poor Herbie clean on to the floor. ' 'Sprivate!'

'Since when did you start keeping a diary?' Angie asked suspiciously.

Daisy blushed. 'Ages ago. No one can look. 'sprivate!'

'OK, OK! Don't bite my head off. I was only curious.'

Wrestling the pillowcases from the pillows with one hand, Angie got on with her work.

Baby Mia rocked and rolled with the motion. Then

she wriggled free from her mum's hip and toddled to pick up Herbie.

'Ah yes, washing-machine for you!' Angie saw the scruffy stuffed hamster and decided he too was for the wash.

'Aw Mum, does he have to?' Daisy fought Mia for possession.

She pulled Herbie's legs while her sister kept strong hold of his head in her podgy fingers. 'He's not even dirty!'

'He's filthy!' Angie decreed.

'But he's already lost one eye in the machine!' Tug-tug-tug.

The truth was, Daisy didn't like to go to sleep without Herbie cuddled up beside her. He was the one who knew all her secrets, the one she planned to read the rest of Miss Ambler's diary to later.

Their mum settled the argument by grabbing Herbie herself.

She whisked the squidgy toy on to the laundry pile, scooped it all up and quickly left the room.

' 'Snot fair!' Daisy yelled.

'Waagh!' Mia cried.

'July 13. Friday.' Daisy snuggled between her clean sheets minus Herbie. She'd taken the diary into the shower in case anyone came across it while she was washing her hair. Now its pages were crinkled and smudged.

Friday the thirteenth! Daisy was superstitious. Surely something really bad and exciting must have happened to Miss Ambler on that day of all days!

'Lost my grandmother's precious diamond ring!' she expected to read. 'Of great sentimental value. The ring was given to her by a mysterious gypsy woman who warned her that if she lost the ring, then she would be forever cursed!' Or, 'Was in town with my friends. Had my Gucci watch stolen from my wrist as we queued outside Angels. The police say it's the work of a gang responsible for a wave of similar snatches in the city centre. They've asked me to work with them as a decoy on future cases. Will discuss it with Mrs Waymann, my headteacher, before I decide to risk my life as gangster bait . . .' Or even, 'Lost a £20 note down a drain. Must be my unlucky day!' But no. What Daisy in fact read was four words. 'Meeting with bank manager.' The real entry was so boring that she practically lost the will to live.

Or at least to stay awake.

"July 14, Saturday – Stayed in. Watched Casualty." Zzzz . . .

'July 15, Sunday – Stayed in. Sewed sacks for sack-race for Wednesday's sports day.' Daisy's head drooped. Boring, boring, boring. Nothing to tell Jimmy except that Miss

Rambler-Ambler washed her hair and went to the dentist like everyone else.

Unless, of course, Daisy used a little imagination and made up one or two harmless, juicy details . . .

Three

'No!'

'Yeah, honest!'

'You're kidding me!'

'No, Jimmy, I'm not. Honest. Miss Ambler did belong to a mega-successful girl-band. Cross my heart and hope to die!'

Daisy hid a grin, her fingers firmly crossed behind her back, then paused at the park gates to borrow Leonie's homework. She made Jimmy lean over, so she could use his scrawny back as a flat surface to scribble Leonie's answers into her own dog-eared maths book.

'Hmm!' Kyle Peterson passed by with Winona,

limping slightly, and wearing a tight bandage around his left knee. 'Looks to me like someone's copying someone else's work!'

'So?' Leonie challenged. With her glorious halo of curly hair, she was a head taller and twice as tough as weedy Kyle.

Winona tilted her head to one side so that a sweep of blonde curls fell across her shoulder. 'Yeah, Kyle; so what?'

Surprised by Winona's fierce interruption, Kyle backed off then walked on with her towards school. 'So, nothing.'

Leonie grinned. 'That Winona; she's got Kyle knocked into shape, no problem!'

Daisy and the gang were finding that the ex-Mizz Perfect had her uses since she'd decided to smash her goody-goody image.

True, Winona was still hard to take sometimes. There was that shampoo-advert hairstyle for a start. And the poor girl still couldn't avoid being a smug know-all as well as the teacher's number one pet. "Winona dear, could you fetch my handbag? . . .Winona, would you run a little errand for me, please?" But basically they now knew where they stood with her.

They were cast-iron certain for instance that she would never let soppy Kyle snitch on Daisy.

'Hurry up!' Jimmy pleaded from beneath Daisy's maths book. His face was turning red with the effort of having to stand in such an awkward, bent position.

'Nearly finished,' she muttered.

Growing bored, Leonie decided to go on ahead. 'See you at school,' she called as she sprang on to a stone wall and ran along the top without faltering. 'Don't mess up my book, OK!'

'This diary . . .' Jimmy said, returning to the earlier subject. 'It definitely – like, *definitely* says that Miss Ambler was a member of a girl-band?'

'Yeah, she had a wild youth,' Daisy insisted straight-faced, polishing off the homework and stuffing both books into her jam-packed schoolbag. Then she gave free rein to her imagination. 'The band was called Iced Melon. They played gigs all over the country; all-night raves, summer rock concerts, that kind of thing.'

'You're joking!' Jimmy double double-checked. His dark-grey eyes grew round and wide in his pointed face. 'What did she do? Play drums . . . or was it keyboard?'

'No. Lead guitar and vocals.' Daisy's mouth quivered at the corners.

Miss Ambler in skin-tight black leather, wailing her way into the Top Twenty. *Sock-it-to-me, sock-it-to-me.*

'Puh!' Jimmy's mouth popped open with a

startled explosion of breath. 'So what's she teaching us lot for, then?'

Daisy shrugged, deciding on a diversion through the park which might make them a minute late for school, but which would take them by the duck-pond. 'Y'know how it is,' she told him, skirting the kids' play area. She swung around the pole of a No-Fouling sign to face him. 'Fame and all that stuff. It doesn't last five minutes. Iced Melon had a number one hit five years ago with "Maybe Tomorrow", then that was it.'

'"Maybe Tomorrow"?' Jimmy racked his brains to remember the monster hit. 'Iced Melon?'

'Forget it,' Daisy recommended. She came to the edge of the pond and stopped to look at a family of speckled brown and yellow ducklings paddling their feet and dabbling their beaks in the murky water. 'Because, listen Jim, there was something even more interesting in Ambler's diary!'

'There was?' Jimmy's eyes lit up, ready for Daisy to dish the dirt on the teacher once more.

She nodded. 'This is top-secret, OK? I mean, it only happened last weekend, so probably nobody knows anything about it yet . . .' Deliberately, Daisy paused. Jimmy was like a fish in a pond, swimming with his mouth open towards the wriggling bait . . .

'. . . No way!'

'Who are you trying to kid?'

'You must be joking, Jimmy!'

Jimmy hadn't been able to wait to break the news about Rambler-Ambler. He mingled with his friends and listened to their reactions as the class filed into assembly.

'Ssh!' Mrs Hunt hissed at Jade, Jared and Maya.

'It's true!' Jimmy insisted. 'Ask Daisy!'

All eyes turned to her. 'Tell you later!' she mouthed back as she reached her place and sat cross-legged on the floor.

'Daisy Morelli, I might have known!' With surprising speed Mrs Hunt leaped from her seat at the side of the hall. With a swing of her skirt and a flurry of fawn pleats, she pounced on Daisy and wagged a finger for her to come out of the row.

'If there's chattering going on during our morning worship, I can be sure to find you at the centre of it!'

Daisy cowered and scowled. She felt like she'd been mauled by a toothless tiger.

'Don't say another word!' Mrs Hunt warned, forcing Daisy to stand by her side as Mrs Waymann the headteacher swept by in a cloud of perfume.

'I didn't . . .' Daisy began.

Mrs Hunt savaged her with a look.

So Daisy faked singing and listening, then openly fidgeted her way through the head's boring notices.

'. . . Winner of the obstacle race: Nathan Moss!' Mrs Waymann announced at last. 'Runner up: Winona Jones!'

The two stood up while the school applauded politely. Only Daisy from her disgraced position saw Legs dozing peacefully in the gap between Nathan's shirt collar and his neck.

Nathan rubbed a hand through his sticky-up hair, then secretly stroked his pet spider, while Winona gave a smug little smile.

'And thank you everyone for helping to make our school sports day such a splendid success!' Mrs Waymann beamed down on her charges, then added an extra notice. 'Now, I'd like a little word with those who kindly stayed behind to help with the clearing up.'

Sixth sense made Jimmy glance quickly and guiltily in Daisy's direction.

She ducked her head, able to guess what was coming next.

The headteacher purred on in a soft, concerned tone of voice.

'Now, if any of you happened across a small black book belonging to Miss Ambler, could you please let a member of staff know where you last saw it?'

Jared, Jade and Maya pressed their lips tight together and stared at the floor.

Leonie slid her neighbour, Jimmy, a curious look.

Winona, Nathan and Kyle felt a small shiver of guilt run along the row.

'The book is important to Miss Ambler,' Mrs Waymann explained, her eyes suddenly darting like an eagle's around the room. No more Mrs Nice Guy. 'Does anyone know anything about it?'

No reply. From Mrs Hunt's side of the hall, Daisy stared straight across at their novice teacher, whose pale face had flushed a bright shade of pink.

There was a long, awkward silence.

'Very well. Dismissed.' Mrs Waymann frowned in disappointment as she left the platform.

And it seemed to Daisy that the head's passing glance caught her and cut through her like a knife.

'Honest, Jimmy; I swear Waymann knows who took the diary!' she whispered at playtime later that morning.

'You didn't *take* it, exactly!' he hissed back.

She darted a narrow look at him, then corrected his slip of the tongue. '*We* didn't take it!'

'OK, **we** didn't take it. It happened by mistake. But what are you gonna do now?'

'What are we gonna do now? Hmm.' Problem. There was the diary, tucked under her mattress at home, safe from prying eyes. Meanwhile, here at school, Waymann would mount an internal investigation to recover it.

'. . . So, Jade Harrison, do you swear that you have nothing whatsoever to do with the disappearance of the vital document?'

Jade, sweating and trembling, would mumble her reply. 'No, miss.'

Curiously, Mrs Waymann suddenly seemed to be

sporting a trim military moustache and wearing a uniform with brass buttons and gold shoulder pads. 'Speak up, girl! If you personally had nothing to do with it, can you at least tell me who did?'

'We have to work out a way of bringing the diary back without anyone knowing it was us,' Daisy decided.

'Yeah, and fast,' Jimmy insisted. He tugged at the short sleeves of his blue football shirt, pulling them down over his skinny elbows until his entire arms disappeared.

'What are you doing? Why aren't you playing football?'

Winona broke in on Daisy and Jimmy's quiet conversation in the corner of the playground.

'Go away, Winona!' Jimmy snapped.

She took no notice. 'And what's this weird stuff I just heard about Miss Ambler?' she said suspiciously.

'What weird stuff?' Daisy countered.

Jared appeared out of nowhere. 'You know!' He winked and grinned. 'You're the ones who told us!'

'About Ambler's love-life!' Maya added, peering out earnestly from behind Jared.

'Miss Ambler's in lu-u-urve!' Jade giggled. She'd shown up as suddenly as the rest. Hot gossip in the far corner, behind the bike-shed. Gossip-alert, gossip-alert!

'Yeah, but this is a joke, isn't it?' Winona turned on Jimmy and cornered him good and proper. 'From what I hear, it can't possibly be true!'

'Why not?'

'It can't be. I mean, Miss Ambler and . . .' Infected by Jade's snorting, spluttering laughter, Winona too began to smile.

'It's true!' Jimmy said hotly. He ducked under Winona's arm and gained the upper hand. Turning back, he shot his hands out from his sleeves and placed them squarely on his hips.

'It was in her diary entry for last Saturday, the fourteenth of July!'

Daisy jumped forward to step smartly on Jimmy's toes. Too late.

Winona stopped giggling and let her mouth fall open. 'What diary? Is that the black book Waymann was on about?'

He nodded. 'Saturday the fourteenth!' Poor, football-mad Jimmy wanted desperately to believe. And he needed to convince the whole school that what Daisy had told him was true. So he turned to her with a pleading look.

'So?' Winona demanded.

Daisy took a deep breath. There was nothing for it; she was in a mess but she would just have to tough this one out. 'So, it's true,' she said. 'Miss Ambler – er, Louise – is in lurve with Jimmy's hero and the Steelers' superstar . . .'

'N-n-no . . . !' Winona stammered.

'Right! Our very own teacher here at Woodbridge Junior is going out with Robbie Exley!'

Four

Before Winona's jaw hit the tarmac in surprise, Daisy obligingly filled in the details.

'Of course, it's early days. They only became an item last Saturday. They met at Angel's nightclub and it was love at first sight.'

'Yeah, yeah!' Winona scoffed.

'It's true!' Jimmy insisted.

Daisy went on. 'Reading between the lines of Louise's secret diary, I would say it's definitely the real thing!'

By this time, Jade and Jared's sneering smiles were starting to fade. Either Daisy was putting on an Oscar-winning performance, or the story was true. Frown marks formed between their eyes, while Daisy went blithely on.

'LURVE, LURVE, LURVE!' she sang, waltzing Winona around the playground. 'Miss Ambler and Robbie Exley. They're gonna get married and have baby footballers. We'll be old enough by then to babysit, and Jimmy will be able to coach all the young Exleys to become great soccer players like their dad!'

Jimmy's eyes lit up. 'Yeah!' he sighed.

'Hmm.' Winona screwed up her mouth. 'Well. I don't believe a word you say.'

'Who cares what you think?' Jimmy jumped in. Boy, did he want his super-hero to be going out with their teacher! 'You didn't even know that Miss Ambler was lead-singer in a girl-band before she was a teacher, so there!'

While Winona's jaw dropped another mile, Daisy edged towards Jimmy. 'Don't push it!' she advised.

In the background, Jade and Jared smiled nervously, waiting to see which way the argument would go.

'Now I *know* you're joking!' Hands on hips, Winona spoke in a sing-song, you-can't-fool-me voice. 'Jimmy Black, if you think for a nano-second that I'm gonna believe that . . . !'

'Yeah!' Jared said, slowly making up his own mind. 'No way!'

Daisy gritted her teeth. This wasn't going well.

'Anyway, I read in my mum's magazine that Robbie Exley's girlfriend is a supermodel called Ingrid,' Jade added.

'That was last week, not this week!' Daisy argued weakly.

'This week he's going out with Ambler!'

Jade and Jared came to join Winona, flanking her on either side. In the distance, Miss Ambler herself came out of the main entrance to ring the handbell which would bring everyone back into school for lessons.

Saved by the bell! Daisy thought with a sigh of relief. She and Jimmy made as if to set off across the playground.

But the other three stood firmly in their way.

'OK, so prove it!' Winona challenged with a toss of her golden head and a flash of her clear grey eyes.

Daisy sidestepped uncertainly. Jimmy stuck out his chin.

'Yeah!' Jade and Jared echoed. 'Prove it!'

'What are we gonna do?' Jimmy asked Daisy on the way home from school that evening.

Daisy had spent the day quietly observing Miss Ambler.

Miss Ambler handing back the maths homework: 'Well done, Leonie. Well done, Nathan. You too,

Winona.' *Smack*! Daisy's book had been slammed down hard on her desk. 'Daisy Morelli, I've never seen such a disgraceful mess in all my life. It looks like Nathan's spider has stepped in some ink and crawled all over the page!'

Wise Daisy had offered no defence. She'd even deliberately miscopied a couple of Leonie's answers to put Ambler off the scent. Full marks and impeccable presentation would've looked suspicious, she knew.

Then Miss Ambler teaching music in the afternoon. *Doh-re-mi*.

Doh-doh-doh! One thing was for sure, Rambler-Ambler's voice was as flat as a pancake. Daisy caught Winona's sneering glance. Like, yeah; lead singer with Iced Melon – not!

And Ambler giving them a talk about school uniform. *Zzzzz*!

'How we look is important. We must be neat and tidy so that we can be a credit to the school when visitors come. Our shirts must be washed and ironed every day, Daisy. We should wear our ties neatly knotted, like Kyle. We should NOT wear our football kit in school, twenty-four hours a day, seven days a week, should we, Jimmy?'

Zzzzzzzz! Daisy had taken the chance to study Miss Boring-Snoring more closely. Her face was round and pale as a Wensleydale cheese, her brown hair long and wispy. And her fashion sense was truly awful: crumpled dark blue skirt, the famous M & S size 12 cream blouse, shapeless and buttoned up to the neck. Flat, black, sensible sandals . . .

Daisy herself was no fashion victim, but even *she* could see that there was nothing about the teacher's appearance that would attract the attention of someone like Robbie Exley.

'I think we should let the whole thing just drop,' she told Jimmy as they stopped on the windy pavement outside his door on Duke Street later that afternoon. 'If we don't mention the Robbie Exley-Miss Ambler thing any more, then Winona and the others will forget it by the weekend.'

Jimmy sniffed, and scuffed the toe of his trainer against the doorstep of Car World. Inside the shop, his dad was stacking aerosol cans into a paint rack, whistling cheerfully as he worked. 'I don't wanna forget it,' he muttered. 'I wanna prove that we're telling the truth.'

Daisy swallowed hard. She ummed and aahed for a while, considering whether or not to break things gently. Like, 'Sorry, Jimmy, I made it all up!' No, that wouldn't work. How about, 'Actually, Jim, I just read another extract from the diary and it says that Robbie finished with Louise on Tuesday night.'? Better. That might work.

'I thought of one way we could prove it,' he insisted. 'Then the whole school would know I wasn't joking.'

'Er, listen . . .' Daisy began.

'No, honest; this is a good idea.' Jimmy was convinced that his plan would work. 'What you have to do is take the diary into school tomorrow. You pretend you just found it in a corner of the cloakroom or something. You take it to Ambler and say the page fell open at the part where it tells you about the nightclub and Robbie Exley. Then you ask her a favour, which she'll do, even if it is her un-favouritist pupil who's asking, because she's so grateful to have her diary back . . .'

As he paused for breath at last, Daisy was able to interrupt.

'And what favour do I ask Miss Ambler for?' she queried.

'Well, this is the good bit!' Jimmy gabbled on, his eyes round with excitement. Standing in front of the shiny window with giant, neon stickers announcing special offers on fast-wax and anti-freeze, he looked

small and innocent. 'You ask Ambler for Robbie's autograph!'

Daisy took a deep breath, hoiked her hair back behind her shoulders and stuffed it inside her shirt collar to stop it blowing in the breeze. 'Right,' she nodded.

'Ambler does what you ask and gives you the signature. That's proof, see. It shows we weren't joking after all!'

Jimmy could twist the knife in when he wanted to.

'Y'see, Herbie; there was this time, ages ago, when Jim and me got to meet Kevin Crowe, the Steelers' manager. Never mind how. I probably told you at the time, but you've forgotten.'

Snuggled in bed beside her, smelling of washing-powder and fresh air, the stuffed hamster kept his one eye firmly on Daisy.

Daisy sighed at the memory of the golden moment. 'Kevin introduced us to Robbie Exley. We actually met him in person. And Robbie signed the back of my T-shirt.'

What's that got to do with the current mess you've got yourself into? Herbie's eye winked in the lamplight as if he was asking Daisy a hard question.

'So, I actually had Robbie's autograph, see. But it was written on my T-shirt. And Mum saw it the moment I walked through the door. Well, you know what she's like about throwing stuff in the washing machine . . .'

I sure do, the squidgy, much-spin-dried hamster seemed to agree.

'Before I could stop her, she'd hauled my clothes off my back and stuck them in the machine on hot-wash. Result: no more autograph. It had faded to nothing. Jimmy nearly went crazy. I had to say sorry hundreds of times before he let it drop.'

Jimmy's soccer-crazy, Herbie reminded her. *To him, Robbie Exley is a footballing god.*

'I know it. So, anyway, today when he had this idea about asking Ambler for Robbie's autograph, he reminded me of how I'd gone and lost it in the washing-machine once before. That cut pretty deep, bringing that thing up all over again . . .'

Which just shows you how much it matters to him. The wise, one-eyed rodent looked deep into Daisy's eyes.

Daisy switched off the light, then turned over in bed, away from Herbie's glassy stare. 'That's just it. I couldn't bear to let him down a second time.'

So?

'So, I said, OK, I'd do it.'

Oh, Daisy!

'I know; stupid, huh? No need to rub it in.'

That's another fine mess you've gotten yourself into.

'Yeah, OK, Herbie. I said lay off, OK!'

With the curtains drawn but the late evening light still filtering through, Daisy knew she was a million miles away from being able to go to sleep. She tossed and turned, rolled into Herbie, still squatting on her pillow, said sorry, moved him to a safe place on her bedside table, then sighed.

'How on earth am I going to do it?' she wondered out loud. 'I mean, think of how mega-embarrassing it's gonna be . . . and what about poor Jimmy?'

Silence from the golden hamster.

Outside the window, a lorry trundled along Duke Street, followed by a motorbike roaring by – *WRROAaaghhh – screeeech – meeyaAAAGHH!*

Daisy shot up in bed. 'Got it!' she cried. 'First thing tomorrow morning, I'll ask Leonie!'

Five

Daisy knew for a fact that Leonie Flowers would understand.

Offer Leonie something naughty and nasty and she would leap on it in a flash. Give her a trick to play, a grown-up to fool, and she was sure to act it out to perfection.

Yet Leonie looked as if butter wouldn't melt, so she never got caught. With her halo of dark curly hair, she was sweet but not *too* sweet. She seemed helpful without being a goody-goody, clever without a trace of geekiness.

That was why everyone in the world wanted to be

best friends with Leonie. And that was the reason why Daisy went to her first thing on Friday to enlist her help.

'This is between you and me, OK?' Daisy insisted.

She'd collared Leonie in the school corridor, between English and PE.

'Cross my heart,' Leonie swore.

'The main thing is, don't breathe a word to Jimmy.'

Leonie nodded. 'Is it about Ambler's diary?'

'Kind of.' One of Daisy's problems was still how to return the stupid, boring thing to its rightful owner. She'd read through to the last entry, desperately searching for a juicy bit of information that was true, but found nothing. Big fat zero. Miss Ambler's life was DULL, DULL, DULL.

SNOOZEVILLE.

So she'd stuffed the diary into the bottom of her schoolbag and now carried it guiltily with her everywhere she went.

'How are you on forging people's signatures?' she asked Leonie in a casual, off-hand way.

Leonie tilted her head to one side. 'Pretty good.'

'Move along, Daisy Morelli!' Mrs Waymann crossed the entrance hallway in a scented cloud which wafted down the corridor along with her cross-sounding voice. 'Why aren't you changed into your PE things like Leonie?'

So Daisy moved along, fishing her trainers out of her bag as they went. 'Whose signatures are you best at?' she inquired.

'Well, Mum and Dad's, obviously,' Leonie admitted. 'And my sister Ariella's, but that's not so good because I don't practise . . .'

Huff-huff-huff!

Distracted, Daisy looked down to see horrid Lennox wheezing and panting down the corridor after them. The fat white dog came padding right up to her school-bag and sniffed hard at her trainers. *Huff-huff*.

'Gerroff, Lennox!' She swung her bag out of reach, managing in her clumsy hurry to tip every item on to the floor.

Splat went an uneaten satsuma from Monday's packed lunch.

Skid went her plastic pencil-case right down the corridor.

Lennox pounced, gnashed the squashed fruit between his drooling chops, tasted it, then spat it back out.

And *flutter-flutter* went Miss Ambler's private diary, last to tip out of the bag and hit the floor.

Snarl-grab! Lennox seized the battered, spattered book.

'Le'go, Lennox!' Daisy wailed.

The bulldog set off at a slow, bow-legged trot down the corridor towards the entrance.

'Lennox, come back!' Daisy's heart thumped. Her

mouth went dry as she saw Bernie King's figure loom large in the main doorway.

'Leave this to me!' Leonie murmured, setting off after the dog. Her long legs easily overtook him before he reached the caretaker and she'd already worked out a foolproof plan.

'Hey, Lennox!' she said coolly, leaning over him with both empty hands hidden behind her back. 'Doggy-choc. Which hand?'

Dumb Lennox was fooled by the promise of food. As his saggy eyes looked up at Leonie's bright, eager face, his jaw slackened and he dropped the diary.

Pant-pant-loll-loll. Doggy-choc. Drool.

Leonie stooped with a grin to pick up the book, which she quickly hid behind her back as Bernie King stomped down the corridor.

Luckily the caretaker was too bent on persecuting Daisy to notice. 'You again!' he hollered as she scrabbled to pick up her pencils and felt-tips. He stared down with disgust at the squashed satsuma which his dog's teeth had mashed. 'I might have known! If there's one person in this school always leaving me a mess to clear up, it's definitely you, Daisy Morelli!'

'So, how about it?' Daisy gasped at Leonie. They were playing a game of pirates during PE, an end-of-term 'treat' which Miss Ambler had forced on the whole class.

They were in the hall with the equipment set out. Foam mats were scattered across the floor between wooden benches and boxes. The overhead beams were lowered and long ropes swung out across the middle of the room. And the aim was for the teams of pirates to cross from one side to the other without being tagged and without setting foot on the floor.

'How about what?' Leonie replied. She'd landed on Daisy's mat with a graceful leap from the end of a swinging rope.

'Forging a signature for me.' Daisy took up from where they'd left off after the Lennox incident.

'Whose?'

'Robbie Exley's!' Daisy hissed.

'. . . You're tagged, Daisy!' Kyle yelled at her from a bench ten feet away. 'I got you. You have to go back to the start!'

Daisy raised her eyebrows and deliberately turned her back.

'Miss, Daisy's cheating!' Kyle called to the teacher, but Jimmy landed on his bench and tagged him so hard that he fell off the bench and drowned in the sea.

'Avast!' Jimmy cried, picturing himself in eye-patch and wooden leg. 'C'mon, me hearties, let's stab the landlubbers through the vitals, aaargh!'

'Let me get this straight.' Leonie frowned at Daisy while pirates swarmed all around. 'You want me to forge Robbie Exley's signature so that you can give it to Jimmy and he can show it as proof that Miss Ambler really is going out with his hero?'

Daisy nodded eagerly. 'You got it!'

'No way.' Leonie shook her head.

'Why not?' Had she heard right? Had Leonie just refused to help? How could this be?

Behind, above and to each side, pirates' blood-curdling yells drowned out the subject of their frantic conversation.

'Take that, you swine!'

'Aagh! Splash! Help, I can't swim!'

'. . . Because,' Leonie hissed back, 'I don't think it'll work!'

'Of course it'll work!' Daisy insisted. 'You forge the signature to look exactly like the real thing, then everyone's happy.'

'Unless someone like brainbox Nathan over there works it out and tells,' Leonie pointed out. 'You know what he's like in SATs tests, getting absolutely everything right?'

'Yeah.' Daisy had to admit that Nathan had a computer for a brain. She could feel her one and only plan slipping from her grasp as Leonie got ready to spring from the mat on to the high beam and swing to the safety of their own ship.

'So?'

'So something like a forged . . .'

'Sshh!' Daisy begged, sneaking a look around the hall.

'. . . signature isn't gonna fool Nathan for a single second.'

So, you're under pressure. Herbie looked calmly out from the top of Daisy's schoolbag. PE had finished. The school day had moved on. He fixed her with his one glass eye. This is a science lesson, isn't it? So, be scientific!

Make a list! Daisy told herself while Miss Ambler demonstrated the way some white stuff turned blue when you heated it on a bunsen burner. After all, a list was scientific:

1. Write to Robbie Exley directly, asking for his signature. (Nope. Robbie must have hundreds of requests just like that. It would take ages for him to get round to sending Daisy what she needed.)

So she crossed out the first idea on the list.

2. Tell Jimmy that Miss Ambler got Robbie's autograph for you, but that fat Lennox came along and

ate it while she wasn't looking. (Hmm. How likely was that? Probably about 4 out of 10. Not good.)

3. Say sorry to Jimmy, but the teacher refused the favour. She said she couldn't possibly take advantage of the fact that she was going out with a famous footballer just to satisfy a pupil's whim. (Better. 6 out of 10. But they would still end up with Nathan, Winona, Kyle etc ripping them to shreds for failing to prove that the story was true.) Daisy sat, pen poised, chewing the plastic end.

Bubble-bubble-crackle-pop! The white stuff on the front bench turned blue. It let off a whiff of foul-smelling smoke.

4. Tell Jimmy that Robbie blistered his writing hand while conducting a chemical experiment, so he couldn't sign any autographs in the foreseeable future . . . (Pathetic. Not even worth writing down.)

Daisy nibbled her pen and pondered.

A nearby whisper from Winona into Nathan's ear made her look up.

'Go ahead, Nathan,' Winona urged, a wicked glint in her eye. 'See what she does!'

Nathan took off his glasses to polish them in a bored way.

Rub-rub in tiny circles with the end of his tie.

'I dare you!' Winona hissed, giggling in the direction of Jade and Jared. 'All you have to say is, "Please Miss, how do you cope with the pressure of having a famous boyfriend?"'

No! Daisy almost yelped the little word out loud. She sat on the edge of her stool as she realised that Winona and Nathan were about to call her bluff.

'Stop fidgeting, Daisy!' Miss Ambler complained without even bothering to look up from her experiment. Her face was flushed with the success of having turned the white powder bright blue.

'Go on, Nathan!' Winona whispered. 'It'll be a laugh!'

'Uh-hum!' Nathan put on his glasses and cleared his throat.

He glanced sideways at Daisy, then at Jimmy sitting two rows in front.

'Yes, Nathan, what is it?' Miss Ambler inquired sweetly, raising her plastic goggles and obviously expecting a difficult science question from her star pupil.

Oh no! This was it! Daisy froze on the edge of her seat.

Exposure. Embarrassment. Shame.

'Please Miss,' Nathan began, his hair sticking up wildly as if he was connected to an electric current. Legs crawled slowly out of the cuff of his shirt sleeve and wandered idly over the chemical formula that Nathan had scribbled in biro on the back of his hand. 'Winona wants to know what it's like going out with a famous boyfriend.'

Six

'Miss, I don't . . . ! Miss, I didn't . . . !' Winona tried to protest.

Daisy squirmed down behind her desk, doing her best to vanish.

Jimmy's shiny face eagerly awaited Miss Ambler's answer.

Nathan sat with a smug grin, not looking at anyone and softly stroking Legs.

The teacher looked for a moment as if she hadn't heard the question. Then, when she realised what Nathan had said, she blushed bright scarlet. 'Nathan, I'm going to pretend that I didn't hear that,' she replied sternly, fixing her goggles back over her eyes and poking about amongst the cindery remains of the blue crystals.

Nathan shrugged then popped Legs into his jam-jar, ready for the end-of-school bell.

Daisy breathed again. At least Miss Ambler's answer hadn't exposed the trick she'd been playing on Jimmy.

But of course the teacher, being a teacher, wasn't prepared to let the subject drop.

'Really, Winona, I'm surprised at you,' Rambler-Ambler grumbled as she gave orders for the pupils to pack their bags. 'I didn't expect you of all people to be involved in such silly stories.'

It was Winona's turn to squirm and blush. But she knew better than to lie and worm her way out. 'Sorry, Miss Ambler.'

'I should think so too.' Casting aside her goggles, the teacher marched purposefully up and down the aisles between the desks. 'What goes on in my private life is my own business, and don't let anyone here suppose otherwise.'

Yeah, bank managers and dentists, blouses and schoolwork; that's all that goes on in Boring-Snoring's private life, Daisy sighed.

'Which brings me to the subject of my missing diary,' Ambler continued, stopping by chance right beside Daisy's desk.

Diary-in-bag. Bag-under-desk. Danger! Danger! Daisy grew hot all over.

The judge sat at his high bench, weighed down by his long white wig. His eyelids were hooded, his nose hooked like a bird of prey's. He fixed his piercing eye on the accused.

'Daisy Morelli, do you continue to deny the charge?'

In the dock, Daisy rattled her leg-irons. Pale and dirty after three months in the dungeon, still she kept her head

high and stared back at her accuser. 'I'm innocent, your majesty, your – er – worship. I never went near no stupid diary!'

The shrivelled old man on the podium dismissed her plea.

'Guilty!' he cackled, banging a wooden hammer on his bench.

'That missing book contains a lot of important information,' Miss Ambler went on, her X-ray gaze seemingly fixed on Daisy's schoolbag. 'There are telephone numbers, appointments and addresses which I can't manage without.'

Mega-cringe! Daisy ducked her head so that her neck disappeared into her hunched shoulders.

'Awright, yer honour, it's a fair cop. But it ain't an 'angin' offence, no way!'

'Take her down to the gallows!' the judge snapped. 'Next!'

Miss Ambler stared at Daisy's bag, then sighed. 'So please, if anyone does happen to come across my diary, be sure to return it to me as soon as possible.'

* * *

'Close!' Jimmy admitted, trotting down the left wing to pick up the ball and take a throw-in. He and Daisy had met up in the park that morning; a soggy Saturday, three days before the end of term. And they'd just been recalling the close call of the previous day.

'I really thought I'd had it!' Daisy confessed.

Saturday meant digging your favourite old T-shirt out of the bottom of the laundry basket, slinging on a pair of shorts and trainers and beating a hasty retreat out of the house before your mum could collar you to look after Mia, or your dad could grab you to mix pizza-dough . . . 'I mean, I could've sworn Ambler could see right through my bag; X-ray eyes – *zzzing*!'

Jimmy raised the ball over his head and aimed down the makeshift pitch. 'You gotta give the diary back!' he insisted.

'I know.' Daisy sped down the centre to collect the throw-in. She dribbled the ball daintily over the rough turf.

'Daisy, Daisy, give us our answer, do!" The crowd roared her on, adapting an ancient popular song. "We're half-crazy, all for the love of you . . . !'

'I'm just waiting for my chance to put it back on Ambler's desk without being seen.'

Jimmy streaked like a whippet from the sideline towards the goal. He received a pass from Daisy and dribbled on. 'Better make it quick,' he advised. 'We've only got three days of school left.'

Jimmy looked up at the goal (two spare trainers neatly placed on the grass), aimed and shot. His ace left foot found the spot. *'Goal!' the fans screamed. 'Yee-eeesss!!!'* Daisy watched Jimmy sprawl to the ground, flip up again and raise both arms to the invisible crowd. She joined him in a victory trot around the empty field. 'What did you do with the ball?' she asked, once the excitement had died down.

'Nothing. It landed in the bottom of the hedge.'

So they trotted behind the goal to search, only to be interrupted by the familiar, breathy snarl of Lennox, the school caretaker's dog.

'Uh-oh!' Daisy muttered. It was never a good thing to meet up with Lennox.

'Here, boy!' Bernie King's voice called from the path beyond the spiky hawthorn hedge.

Ignoring his lord and master, Lennox found Jimmy's ball and promptly sank his fangs into it.

Hiss! Daisy and Jimmy watched in dismay as the dog's teeth punctured their football.

'Hey!' Jimmy cried, about to wrestle with the wheezy bulldog.

Daisy pulled him back. 'What's the point? The ball's useless.'

Ducking through a gap in the hedge, they glowered at Lennox, who by this time had waddled off with the ruined ball and dropped it at his owner's size eleven feet.

'Tutt-ttt!' Bernie shook his head and looked at Daisy as if it was all her fault. Like, *Can't a man walk his dog without some brainless twerp kicking a ball in our direction?* 'Now, if you want to know about a kid with real footballing talent, you should meet my nephew, William,' he began.

William-this. William-that.

For five whole minutes King blocked the path with his broad figure and went on and on about the miraculous soccer talent of his brother's son.

'William King. He's Barry's boy. You might've heard of him?'

'Nope,' Daisy replied, determined not to listen. All

she wanted to do was to retrieve their mashed ball and get out of the drizzling rain that had begun to fall.

'Kevin Crowe just signed him up for the Steelers' youth squad. It was in all the newspapers. He's only seventeen years old, yet they're calling William the best goalkeeping prospect England has had since Gordon Banks in '66.'

'That's fantastic!' Jimmy gasped, utterly impressed by the idea of Bernie's nephew rubbing shoulders with the stars.

'Does he train with the first team players?'

King nodded proudly. 'Yeah, our William's hobnobbing with the likes of Hans Kohl and Pedro Martinez.'

'Robbie Exley?' Jimmy added hopefully.

'C'mon, Jim, let's go!' Daisy tugged at the sleeve of her friend's football shirt, uneasy at the turn of the conversation.

But Jimmy was talking about his one and only passion. He dug in his heels and waited for a reply.

The off-duty caretaker took out a yellow, rolled-up kagoul and struggled into it. Then he nodded again. 'As a matter of fact, Robbie Exley and his girlfriend took our William out clubbing last weekend.'

'Wow!' Jimmy sighed. 'How about that for a coincidence? Last weekend was the first date for Robbie and ...*ouch*!'

Pretending to dive for the flattened ball which Lennox had slobbered all over and finally dropped, Daisy cannoned into Jimmy and stopped him mid-sentence.

Bernie King didn't notice. He just went on boasting about his precious nephew. 'Yes,' he nodded, spraying raindrops from the hood of his kagoul. 'Robbie and Ingrid took our William to Angels nightclub in the centre of town.'

Daisy groaned and sighed.

'Ingrid?' Jimmy interrupted with a puzzled frown. 'Ingrid who?'

'Oh, Ingrid whatsits . . .' King struggled to remember.

'You know, that blonde supermodel from Sweden. She and Robbie have been seeing each other for the past six months.'

'You made the whole thing up!' Jimmy's accusation rang across the rainy park.

He and Daisy had left Bernie King and Lennox to the rest of their damp walk and ducked back through the hedge.

Now he turned to face her with a look of shocked realisation.

'You lied to me, Daisy. Miss Ambler isn't Robbie Exley's girlfriend at all. She probably doesn't even *know* him!'

Daisy hung her head. The soaking rain had plastered her hair to her face. She shivered inside her wet T-shirt.

'Does she?' Jimmy insisted.

'No.'

He was pale with anger. 'And that means you can't get Robbie's autograph either, can you?'

'No,' she whispered again. She'd let down her best friend, made a fool of him and turned him against her.

Taking a deep breath, he grabbed the deflated ball from her, tucked it under his arm and got ready to sprint off. 'Just you wait, Daisy Morelli!' he yelled at her. 'I mean it; just you wait and see!'

Seven

'Why so gloomy, Daisy *mia*; just like this 'orrible English weather?' Gianni had asked.

All Saturday and Sunday she'd gone around the flat and restaurant with a long face.

'What happened to Jimmy today?' Angie had inquired.

'Mum, that's the fourth time you've asked me,' Daisy had snapped back. 'I don't have to do *everything* with him, do I?'

Even Herbie posed awkward questions. *You know this is all your fault, don't you, Daisy? If you hadn't made up the diary entries in the first place, none of this would have happened.*

Daisy shoved the hamster down to the bottom of her bag as she got ready for school on the Monday morning. *Oh, and by the way; about this diary . . .* She'd velcroed the bag tight shut to stop him from finishing.

And what had Jimmy meant by yelling 'Just you wait!' at her across the rain-soaked pitch? The problem filled her head as she trudged towards Woodbridge Road.

Did he mean, for instance, that he would never speak to her again? Or that he would find a more sneaky way of getting his own back?

What if, just for example, Jimmy decided to drop Daisy in it over Ambler's diary?

She felt a jolt in her chest as her heart missed a beat. Then she picked up her pace to arrive at school before Jimmy did.

She would have to plead with him, go down on her knees and beg him not to tell. (*I wouldn't blame him if he did,* Herbie grunted from the depths of her bag.) 'Hey, Daisy!' Jade called as she sped through the big iron gates.

Daisy waved and ran on. 'Have you seen Jimmy?' she gasped at Jared, who stood on the top step under the main entrance.

'No, he's not here yet,' he told her. 'He was still having his breakfast when I called at his house.'

'Thank heavens!' Daisy relaxed and collapsed on to the step, dumping her bag beside her.

Nathan, who had sloped silently up the steps after

her, had his head in a different universe as usual. Probably the world of black holes and other space mysteries which defied the laws of physics. Anyway, he tripped over Daisy's bag and sent Legs spiralling on an invisible thread towards the floor.

'Daisy Morelli, pick up that bag before someone breaks a leg!' Mrs Gloom-and-Doom Hunt wailed from inside the building.

'Here comes Jimmy now,' Jared warned from his lookout point. 'He's got Leonie, Winona and Kyle with him. And he's waving a piece of paper in their faces. What's going on?'

Already on her feet, Daisy followed Jared across the playground. She noticed that Jimmy wore a grin spreading from ear to ear, without a trace of the shock he'd displayed when she'd confessed the rotten Miss Ambler-Robbie Exley trick to him.

'Talk about lucky!' Leonie sighed, grabbing the paper from Jimmy and reading a long list of names. 'Wow, Jimmy, this is totally A-MAZING!'

'What is?' Daisy pestered, pushing in between Leonie and Jimmy. The list looked like signatures; about a dozen names scrawled haphazardly down the page. 'Jimmy, what is it?'

'Nothing!' he retorted, staring down his snub-nose at her.

He grabbed the paper back from Leonie before

Daisy had chance to read it.

'A-MAZING!' Winona echoed with an admiring sigh. She turned to Daisy. 'Jimmy only went and got Robbie Exley's autograph like he said!'

'What . . . ? How . . . ?' Daisy stuttered.

Jimmy flashed her a Cheshire-cat grin, cheesy and mysterious.

'I asked Miss Ambler, like we planned!' he said innocently.

Liar! Daisy shot back a vicious look. But she couldn't breathe a word out loud. *(Well, you lied to him first*, old Herbie remarked from her bag on the top step.)

'AND he's got autographs from the entire first team!' Kyle added. 'Hans Kohl . . . Pedro Martinez, plus Kevin Crowe!'

'Never, Jimmy! You must be joking!' Daisy gasped. She felt her legs go weak. Surely he couldn't have . . . wouldn't have . . . no, definitely not!

But then again, how else could Jimmy have the set of twelve signatures if he hadn't sat and faked the whole blooming lot?

'And today, Class 5A, we're in for a big surprise!' Miss Ambler stood at the front of the room and promised the group a special end of term treat.

No, I can't take any more surprises! Daisy groaned inwardly.

First, there was Jimmy and his set of 'autographs'. Huh, what a way to get his own back; forging all twelve signatures! Daisy had sulked her way through assembly.

And second, there was the unbelievable vision of Miss Ambler dressed to kill.

'She's wearing make-up!' Jade had sniggered as the teacher walked in to take registration.

'She's streaked her hair!' Winona whispered, stunned by the complete makeover. 'And that's a designer label shirt!'

'Look at those shoes; trendy or what!' Maya spoke up from her corner at the back of the class.

'Never mind the shoes; what about the trousers?' Kyle pointed out the skin-tight pair clinging to Miss Ambler's legs.

New clothes, hair-dye, make-up, perfume – the full works for Louise. What had got into their mouse-like teacher?

'Would you like to know what the surprise is?' Ambler asked, teetering on her high heels, teasing them.

'Yes - yes - yes!' the whole class begged.

'Well, you all remember Nathan's cheeky remark about my famous boyfriend,' she began coyly.

'Yes, miss!' All the kids held their breaths.

Daisy could hear the cogs inside her brain slowly grinding and crunching. 'Famous boyfriend'? But wasn't that purely the product of Daisy's own over-heated imagination? Hadn't she made it all up inside her head?

'As you know, I don't like to drag my personal life into school with me,' Miss Ambler went on, 'but since Nathan somehow blew my cover, as you might say, I thought I might as well use my connections (*nudge-nudge, wink-wink*) to give you all a treat.'

'Wow! Cool! C'mon, Miss, tell us!'

Daisy glared at Jimmy, whose eyes had glazed over and whose grin had grown fixed on his pointed face.

'All in good time,' their newly-glamorous teacher assured them. 'Let's just say that it may have something to do with your favourite football team. Meanwhile, I'm enjoying keeping the secret.'

'Aw, Miss! Please, Miss!'

Her glossy lips smiled as she turned her head to look out of the window at a low, sporty silver car which had just swung into the playground. 'Look outside!' she whispered.

So they stood and craned their necks, Jimmy and Daisy along with all the rest.

They watched the gleaming doors open. They gasped once, then twice as two men stepped out of the car.

Daisy leaned forward to the desk in front to grab Jimmy's blue shirt. 'Did you set this up?' she hissed, her head in a complete spin.

Jimmy shook his head. 'Search me!'

The two men sauntered towards the entrance, hands in tracksuit pockets.

'Then, how . . . ?' Daisy stuttered.

Jimmy tugged free and turned on her. 'Listen, I admit that I went behind your back to get the autographs!' he hissed. 'I couldn't resist; I just wanted to see your face when I brought them in.'

'Hmm. So how did you get them?'

'Easy. I went round to Bernie King's flat on Saturday lunchtime, knowing there was a benefit match between the firsts and the junior squad in the afternoon. So I asked Bernie if he would ask William to get the whole first team and the Steelers manager to give me their autographs. He told me, sure; anything for a genuine fan like me. It was as simple as that!'

'Jammy!' Daisy breathed. She gazed out of the window through narrowed eyes. 'But you're sure you didn't have anything to do with this?'

The buzz of excitement inside the classroom rose as the unexpected guests entered the building. Chairs scraped, kids crowded towards the door.

'Swear, cross my heart and hope to die!' Jimmy insisted.

Major mystery.

Because it was Steelers' manager, Kevin Crowe, opening the door and walking into the classroom.

And, behind him, with rays of sunlight falling on his messy haircut and with a shy grin on his handsome, square face was Super-Rob, top goal-scorer in the Premiership, national hero and demi-god.

'. . . Ohhhhhhhhhh!' the whole class gasped.

Miss Ambler smiled and went forward to greet the star.

Robbie Exley smiled back. He embraced the teacher and kissed her on the cheek.

Eight

Am I dreaming? Daisy stood with her mouth open. Robbie Exley had just kissed Miss Ambler.

OK, so it had only been on the cheek. But it *was* in front of the whole class.

The teacher smiled and embraced the soccer star.

Daisy blinked, then glanced at a gobsmacked Jimmy.

Weak at the knees, Jimmy sat down hard at his desk. 'ROB-BIE EX-LEY!' he mouthed, eyes shining, cheeks flushed.

Robbie and Kevin in their very own school, wearing flash Steelers tracksuits, windswept and glowing as if they'd come straight from the training ground.

The door opened again. Thirty two heads turned to see a tall blonde woman enter the room. Thin and tanned, with her hair pulled back and sprouting carelessly from a sparkly clasp, she glided towards Miss Ambler.

'Hey, Louise,' she said casually in a thick foreign accent.

Then she too hugged and kissed the teacher.

'Ingrid Salminen!' Wannabe Winona gasped, so loud that everybody heard. She noted every detail of the supermodel's styling so that she could go home and practise in the mirror later.

Help! a small voice inside Daisy's head cried.
What's going on?

Emerging from the elegant embrace, Miss Ambler smiled at the class. 'I take it that our visitors need no introduction. But in case anyone is still wondering, I'd like you to meet Ingrid Salminen and Robbie Exley.'

As she spoke, the two superstars linked up. Lovey-dovey, hands around waists, smiling warmly into each others' eyes.

No! Wait! Action replay! First Robbie was kissing and hugging Miss Ambler. Now he was making out that he and Ingrid were still an item. Daisy couldn't work it out.

'And this is my friend, Kevin Crowe,' Miss Ambler

went on shyly. 'I'm sure you all recognise him from his appearances on *'TV Sport'*.'

Kevin chose that moment to step forward from the shadow of Robbie and Ingrid's golden glory. He grinned at the rows of stunned faces. And then, unbelievably, he slipped his own arm around their teacher's waist.

'See, she *did* have a famous boyfriend!' Nathan pointed out in his smarmiest know-all voice.

The playtime bell had gone and a gaggle of kids from 5A were gathered around the gate from where they'd waved off their superstar visitors.

Robbie and Kevin had answered a load of eager questions and told funny stories about the world of soccer. Robbie had grinned sheepishly but refused to show the class his shoulder tattoo. Then, finally, the famous three had said goodbye.

'And thank you for making this a very special day at Woodbridge School!' Miss Ambler had spoken for everyone.

Ingrid and Robbie had signed autographs, while Kevin had chatted quietly with the teacher. He'd kissed her and given her a squeeze on the way out.

'No wonder she didn't deny it,' Winona added.

'Wasn't that mega mega mega mega mega mega cool!' Jimmy sighed, eking out the last glimpse of the silver car as it slid around the corner. All the confusion and betrayal of the last few days had melted away in the glory of the moment.

'Daisy, wasn't that the coolest?'

'Yeah, cool,' she muttered, still reeling from the shock. No wonder Miss Ambler had glammed up for the occasion. If Kevin had seen her in her workaday cream blouse and blue skirt, he might well have changed his mind about going out with her!

And the teacher had scrubbed up well, Daisy had to admit.

But really, Nathan was a pain, going on about things the way he was.

'Only one problem,' he smirked. 'The famous boyfriend turns out NOT to be Robbie Exley, like Daisy claimed!'

The whole gang took in what Nathan said. They bunched up their mouths and narrowed their eyes.

'Hey, yeah!' Jared said slowly.

'How come?' Maya asked.

Winona stepped up close. 'Yeah, Daisy; how come?'

Frantically Daisy looked for an answer. She turned to Jimmy, who was still sighing and drooling over the visit. No help there. 'I must've read it wrong in Miss Ambler's diary,' she muttered weakly.

'Typical!' Nathan poured scorn on her excuse. He pushed his glasses more firmly on to his nose. 'Now, if you'd just bothered to read more carefully, you'd have soon seen that Miss Ambler was going out with Kevin Crowe. It's there in black and white.'

Flip-flop. Daisy's heart turned over. How could Nathan possibly know? Unless he'd ferreted around in Daisy's bag and discovered the secret black book. Wait a second; didn't she recall Nathan hanging about on the step by the main entrance earlier that morning? Yeah; he'd tripped over the bag just before she and Jared had run off to meet Jimmy. And, disaster – she'd left the bag on the step for anyone to rummage through . . .

Oh no! *Flip-flop-flap*! Daisy's stomach heaved and rolled as she silently split away from the gang and sped back into school.

Jimmy and Nathan followed more slowly with knowing looks.

'Daisy Morelli, get out!' Mrs Hunt waylaid her by the cloakroom. 'It's dry-play. You're not allowed in school!'

Daisy ducked around the corner and sped on. She'd have to face Moaning Minnie later, no doubt. But she needed to find her bag. It was a matter of life and death.

Zooming down the corridor, heart thumping and mouth dry, Daisy made it to the classroom. She flung open the door, then wove through rows of desks to reach her own.

There was her bag, hanging half-empty on the back

of her chair. She ripped open its velcro fastening and delved inside. Her groping fingers made contact with her lunch-box, her pencil-case, a pair of dead socks . . .

'Daisy?' Miss Ambler asked from the stock-room door.

Daisy jumped back guiltily. No diary! Definitely no diary in the bag!

'Are you sure you're all right?' the teacher wiggled towards her on her high heels.

'Fine!' Daisy squeaked. Not only no diary, but no Herbie either! Both book and hamster were missing.

'You don't look well,' Miss Ambler insisted in a concerned voice. 'Has the excitement of the morning been too much?'

'Yes, Miss. I suppose so, Miss.' OK, so Nathan had snuck behind her back and stolen the diary. But what for? It didn't make any sense, unless, unless . . .

'Stop that dog!' Nathan's shout echoed down the corridor.

'Jimmy, grab that book from Lennox before he chews it to bits!'

Huff-huff-huff! Fat Lennox panted and pounded past the classroom.

Or at least, Miss Ambler and Daisy were meant to think he did.

Clicking into action while the teacher stood marooned in the middle of the room, Daisy dashed to the door in time to see not Lennox, but Jimmy

crouching low and imitating the bulldog's wheeze. *Huff-huff! Grrraaggh!*

'Got it!' Jimmy growled, then held up the scruffy book.

'Well done!' Nathan congratulated him. 'Miss Ambler will be pleased that we've got her diary back!'

Huff-huff-huff . . . Jimmy pretended to be Lennox thundering off down the corridor.

'My diary?' Miss Ambler came up behind Daisy, in time to see Nathan and Jimmy hurrying in triumph towards her.

'Lennox had it all the time!' Nathan exclaimed with a sideways, smug look at Daisy. 'He must have grabbed it and run off with it after sports day. No wonder it looks so chewed up!'

* * *

'The dog ate Ambler's diary!' Jimmy announced with a wide grin, back in the playground before the end of break.

Things had happened fast and Daisy was only just beginning to recover. The teacher had been deeply grateful to Jimmy and Nathan. Daisy herself was off the hook at last.

'Yeah, yeah!' Jade, Jared, Maya and Winona smirked. 'Fat Lennox is innocent. Free Fat Lennox!'

'Well, Ambler thinks he did,' Nathan confirmed, 'and that's what matters.' Then he turned to Daisy. 'No need to thank me!' he crowed.

'I wasn't going to . . .' she muttered.

'Anyway, I was acting under orders. I only sneaked the diary out of your bag and set up the Lennox trick because Jimmy told me to.'

Daisy turned slowly to her friend. 'Jimmy?'

He shrugged his skinny shoulders. 'Yeah, well, someone had to do something to help you out of the hole you'd got yourself into. And I knew if I involved Nathan, Ambler would believe anything he said.'

'Clever!' Winona nodded. 'Good thinking, Jim.'

The trick had sent Jimmy's reputation rocketing sky-high.

'And what about Herbie?' Daisy demanded, crossing her arms in a giant huff. 'Why did you have to nick him too?'

Jimmy rolled his eyes towards Nathan. He spread his hands palms upwards. 'I don't know what you're talking about!'

'Yes, you do! Herbie's gone missing. You told Nathan to steal him!'

Jimmy's eyebrows shot up under his fringe, all innocent. 'Me?'

'Yes, you! To get your own back!'

Winona, Jared and the rest tuned in with fresh interest. A row between Jimmy and Daisy? This was something new.

'What for?' Jimmy pretended to be puzzled.

'You know!' For lying to him about the diary entry. But the others didn't know about that. And Jimmy knew that Daisy knew that they didn't know . . . Daisy got lost in the maze of pretence and gave up.

'I wouldn't worry about Herbie,' he teased, grinning at geeky Nathan. 'I guess he just went for a walk around school.'

'He's a stuffed toy!' Winona reminded everyone. She was a girl with no visible sense of humour. 'How can he wander off?'

Jimmy tossed his fringe back, shrugged, but said nothing.

Daisy fumed and fretted.

Serves you right! said Herbie, tucked securely into Jimmy's waistband beneath the oversized football shirt. Frankly, he refused to lift a paw to help.

Jimmy grinned and practised a dodging dribble around Daisy, his flat-footed opponent. 'Herbie will show up,' he assured her wickedly. 'All in his own good time!'